CHRISTMAS KISSES

SOUL SISTERS AT CEDAR MOUNTAIN LODGE, BOOK 2

JUDITH KEIM

PRAISE FOR JUDITH KEIM'S NOVELS

THE BEACH HOUSE HOTEL SERIES

"Love the characters in this series. This series was my first introduction to Judith Keim. She is now one of my favorites. Looking forward to reading more of her books."

BREAKFAST AT THE BEACH HOUSE HOTEL *is an easy, delightful read that offers romance, family relationships, and strong women learning to be stronger. Real life situations filter through the pages. Enjoy!"*

LUNCH AT THE BEACH HOUSE HOTEL *– "This series is such a joy to read. You feel you are actually living with them. Can't wait to read the latest one."*

DINNER AT THE BEACH HOUSE HOTEL *– "A Terrific Read! As usual, Judith Keim did it again. Enjoyed immensely. Continue writing such pleasantly reading books for all of us readers."*

CHRISTMAS AT THE BEACH HOUSE HOTEL *– "Not Just Another Christmas Novel. This is book number four in the series and my introduction to Judith Keim's writing. I wasn't disappointed. The characters are dimensional and engaging. The plot is well crafted and advances at a pleasing pace. The Florida location is interesting and warming. It was a delight to read a romance novel with mature female protagonists. Ann and Rhoda have life experiences that enrich the story. It's a clever book about friends and extended family. Buy copies for your book group pals and enjoy this seasonal read."*

THE HARTWELL WOMEN SERIES – Books 1 – 4

"This was an EXCELLENT series. When I discovered

Judith Keim, I read all of her books back to back. I thoroughly enjoyed the women Keim has written about. They are believable and you want to just jump into their lives and be their friends! I can't wait for any upcoming books!"

"I fell into Judith Keim's Hartwell Women series and have read & enjoyed all of her books in every series. Each centers around a strong & interesting woman character and their family interaction. Good reads that leave you wanting more."

THE FAT FRIDAYS GROUP – Books 1 – 3

"Excellent story line for each character, and an insightful representation of situations which deal with some of the contemporary issues women are faced with today."

"I love this author's books. Her characters and their lives are realistic. The power of women's friendships is a common and beautiful theme that is threaded throughout this story."

THE SALTY KEY INN SERIES

FINDING ME – *"I thoroughly enjoyed the first book in this series and cannot wait for the others! The characters are endearing with the same struggles we all encounter. The setting makes me feel like I am a guest at The Salty Key Inn...relaxed, happy & light-hearted! The men are yummy and the women strong. You can't get better than that! Happy Reading!"*

FINDING MY WAY- *"Loved the family dynamics as well as uncertain emotions of dating and falling in love. Appreciated the morals and strength of parenting throughout. Just couldn't put this book down."*

FINDING LOVE – *"I waited for this book because the*

first two was such good reads. This one didn't disappoint.... Judith Keim always puts substance into her books. This book was no different, I learned about PTSD, accepting oneself, there is always going to be problems but stick it out and make it work. Just the way life is. In some ways a lot like my life. Judith is right, it needs another book and I will definitely be reading it. Hope you choose to read this series, you will get so much out of it."

FINDING FAMILY – *"Completing this series is like eating the last chip. Love Judith's writing, and her female characters are always smart, strong, vulnerable to life and love experiences."*

"This was a refreshing book. Bringing the heart and soul of the family to us."

CHANDLER HILL INN SERIES

GOING HOME – *"I absolutely could not put this book down. Started at night and read late into the middle of the night. As a child of the '60s, the Vietnam war was front and center so this resonated with me. All the characters in the book were so well developed that the reader felt like they were friends of the family."*

"I was completely immersed in this book, with the beautiful descriptive writing, and the authors' way of bringing her characters to life. I felt like I was right inside her story."

COMING HOME – *"Coming Home is a winner. The characters are well-developed, nuanced and likable. Enjoyed the vineyard setting, learning about wine growing and seeing the challenges Cami faces in running and growing a business. I look forward to the next book in this series!"*

"Coming Home was such a wonderful story. The author has such a gift for getting the reader right to the heart of things."

HOME AT LAST – "a beautiful conclusion to this fantastic series with family as a strong foundation"

SEASHELL COTTAGE BOOKS

A CHRISTMAS STAR – "Love, laughter, sadness, great food, and hope for the future, all in one book. It doesn't get any better than this stunning read."

"A Christmas Star *is a heartwarming Christmas story featuring endearing characters. So many Christmas books are set in snowbound places...it was a nice change to read a Christmas story that takes place on a warm sandy beach!" Susan Peterson*

CHANGE OF HEART – "CHANGE OF HEART is the summer read we've all been waiting for. Judith Keim is a master at creating fascinating characters that are simply irresistible. Her stories leave you with a big smile on your face and a heart bursting with love."

~Kellie Coates Gilbert, author of the popular Sun Valley Series

A SUMMER OF SURPRISES – "Judith Keim at her best… this book will be the best of the Summer/beach read." J.C. Amazon

CHRISTMAS KISSES

SOUL SISTERS AT CEDAR MOUNTAIN LODGE, BOOK 2

JUDITH KEIM

Published in the United States by:
Wild Quail Publishing
P.O. Box
Boise, Idaho 83717

ISBN #978-1-954325-46-3
FIRST EDITION

This book is dedicated to women everywhere who connect with others, becoming sisters of the heart—soul sisters

Coming Home – A Chandler Hill Inn Book – 2

Home at Last – A Chandler Hill Inn Book – 3

Winning BIG – a little love story for all ages

Hailey Bennett sat in the cozy kitchen wondering how to begin. Mrs. Kirby, her new foster mother, had asked her and the other three girls in the house to write a letter to Santa. She tapped the pencil against the wooden tabletop, trying to form the words in her head.

She'd learned at school that writing words was easier for her than talking. Talking sometimes got her into big trouble. Besides, she liked the words and people she made up and kept inside her head. These characters all lived in fancy big houses with a Mom and a Dad who loved them. Not in houses where yelling and hitting took place. Her teacher told her she had a great imagination and that someday she could become an excellent storyteller. Maybe. Now, she'd better pretend she believed in Santa. She looked around. The other girls were busy writing to him. She wondered if she could make the words come out right.

She began to form the printed letters on paper as carefully as she could.

"Dear Santa, I want a pupy for Xmas with lots of kisses.

Your frind,
Hailey Bennett."

"How are you doing, sweetheart? Need any help?" Mrs. Kirby asked, coming into the kitchen and giving her a friendly smile.

Hailey shook her head. She knew better than to bring attention to herself. That had only caused a slap or a nasty remark in the foster home she'd just left. Those people were called out of town for the holidays to take care of a sick relative. Or so the person from Foster Care Services told her. They'd left without even saying goodbye to her. Another house that didn't work for her.

At the memory of finding herself alone again, tears escaped her eyes and dropped onto the lenses of her eyeglasses. She quickly took them off and rubbed them dry. She didn't want the other girls to see. They might call her a crybaby, like the kids at school sometimes did. Or "four-eyes," which was almost as bad.

Hailey left the kitchen and joined the older girls in the family room. Carefully, so as not to draw attention to herself, she sat on the floor by the doorway. From here, she wouldn't bother anyone. It was a good place to make up some of her favorite stories.

At eight, she'd lived through a lot of disappointments, and these stories brought her comfort.

Hailey studied the lights on the Christmas tree and listened to the holiday music. Soon she became lost in a memory of colorful lights, a soft voice, and blue eyes. She'd been told her mother had died when she was four, and they didn't know how to find her father. She thought it must be a mistake. Somewhere her mother was looking for her. She was sure of it. When she got old enough, she'd go find her.

Mrs. Kirby came and sat down beside her. She had long brown hair and dark-brown eyes. Kind eyes. "Pretty Christmas lights, huh?"

Hailey nodded.

"I hope you'll be comfortable here with me and the other girls. Anytime you need to talk to me about something, feel free to do it. Okay?"

Hailey studied her and then nodded. This new foster mother seemed really nice, but only time would tell if this house would be the right one.

"I have something for you," Mrs. Kirby said. "Something to welcome you."

Hailey felt her eyes widen. This was something new.

"Would you like to open it now?" Mrs. Kirby's eyes sparkled with excitement.

Her pulse speeding up with excitement she didn't dare show, Hailey bobbed her head up and down.

Mrs. Kirby got to her feet, went into her downstairs bedroom, and returned with a gaily-wrapped package. "Here. This is for you."

Hailey accepted the gift and held it to her chest. "Mine?"

"Yes, yours," Mrs. Kirby said, patting her shoulder. "Go ahead and open it."

Hailey carefully unwrapped the package, slowly lifted the paper off, and stared with disbelief at the stuffed puppy dog. The brown fur felt soft as she lifted it into her arms. Dark- brown, button eyes stared deep inside her to where she hid her feelings. The pink-felt tongue sewn into the mouth looked as if it wanted to kiss her.

"Mine?" Hailey said again, needing to be sure. It was the closest she'd ever come to having something like this of her own.

"Yes, sweetie, it's yours. Later, after the holidays, we'll get a real dog in the house. But all of us will have to decide together on what kind it'll be."

Hailey buried her face into the puppy's soft fur and felt her eyes fill. This time, words inside her head weren't enough. "I ... I love it," she managed to say. Her lips trembled with emotion.

Hailey noticed Mrs. Kirby's eyes grow as watery as her own. "This dog will help you. Any time you feel uncomfortable, Hailey, bring him to me, and we'll talk to him and you about it. Okay?"

Hailey thought for a moment, and nodded, trying not to be a big crybaby.

Throughout the rest of the evening, Hailey held the dog close to her.

One of the girls saw her and asked, "What's your puppy's name?"

Hailey shrugged, too shy to answer.

"How about Charlie, for Charlie Brown?"

Hailey giggled and nodded. "Okay."

She hugged the dog. *Hi, Charlie.*

Hailey spent the next few days taking in every detail of her new surroundings and studying the other girls, Charlie constantly in tow. By now, Hailey knew the oldest girl was a dark-haired girl named Jo. The other two were Alissa, a girl not much bigger than she who had big brown eyes, and red-haired Stevie. As Mrs. Kirby explained, they'd all been in need of a new home too. Hailey studied them and held onto her dog, wondering what life would be like here. Already, it might be the best ever.

Some things might take her a while to get used to though. Like how tonight Mrs. Kirby took her hand after dinner and cheerily announced, "Time for a bath and to get ready for bed."

Hailey wasn't used to someone holding her hand. Not in a nice way.

Mrs. Kirby led her upstairs, chatting quietly about the good day they'd had. Hailey was sharing a room with Alissa. Mrs. Kirby, or Maddie as one of the big girls called her, had figured the two of them, as the youngest, wouldn't mind sharing, that it would be nice for them to know they weren't alone. Hailey was glad. She clutched Charlie to her chest, glad, too, she had Charlie to make her feel safe.

Okay, Charlie, bath time.

Upstairs, Mrs. Kirby led her into a big room at the front of the house. Though it was getting dark outside, Hailey could see the soft glow of street lights through the large window that gave a nice view of the pretty neighborhood.

Hailey noticed Mrs. Kirby looking around the room sadly, and reached out and touched her hand.

Mrs. Kirby's eyes widened and then filled with tears. She knelt on the floor and wrapped her arms around Hailey, filling her with a warm feeling. "Ah, Hailey, you're such a sweetie. I hope you're going to be happy here."

Wanting to please Mrs. Kirby, Hailey nodded, though she was waiting to be told she'd have to move. Again.

Mrs. Kirby rose and patted her on the head. "I have another surprise. Here is your new Christmas nightgown. All the girls got them."

Hailey stared at the red flannel nightgown whose collar and cuffs were edged in lace. It was beautiful. "Mine?" she asked, touching the soft, warm fabric.

"Yes, yours, Hailey. After your bath, we'll put it on and hopefully I'll have time for a short story with you and Alissa before I need to get the other girls settled."

In a daze of disbelief, Hailey took her bath, put on her new nightgown, and climbed into her soft, clean bed, the one closest to the window. Alissa, a nice girl who sometimes let her hold her unicorn pillow, slept in the other bed. She liked having Alissa in the same room.

After both girls were tucked in, Mrs. Kirby sat down on the edge of Hailey's bed with a couple of books. Hailey grinned at Alissa. Of all the things that would make this day even more magical it was having a story read to them.

As Mrs. Kirby read aloud a book about a moon and another story about a girl moving to a new home, a peace settled inside Hailey. She had a new home too.

The next day, Mrs. Kirby surprised her by saying, "We're going shopping so you can get gifts for the other girls in the house. It's Christmas Eve, and we don't have much time for you to choose something for them and get it wrapped."

Hailey simply stared at her. She'd never bought a gift or wrapped a gift or even thought of Christmas this way.

"If you've never done this before, that's okay!" said Mrs. Kirby. "I'll help you decide what to get if you need me to. Don't worry, it's going to be fun. This is what Christmas is all about—thinking of others, having fun, and remembering to be grateful for all you have."

Hailey forced words out of her head into her mouth. "Thank you. That will be fun."

Mrs. Kirby smiled. "I think so too."

Later, at the store, Hailey squeezed a five-dollar bill in her hand and hugged Charlie closer to her. The store was alive with activity as people strolled the aisles, and Christmas music played through loud-speakers. Nearby, Mrs. Kirby said, "Remember, choose something you think each of the girls would like. Something you might like yourself, perhaps. I know you've just met them, but knowing you, I'm sure you'll come up with something special for each of them."

Hailey had studied each of the girls in the house. Some choices would be easy. Some not. Charlie would help her.

It took her no time to choose a book for Alissa. She'd loved their story time as much as Hailey. For Stevie, she finally chose a notebook with a picture of a fox on it. Stevie seemed to have words in her head too. Jo was the hardest choice of all. She seemed tough, but Hailey knew better. She walked slowly up one aisle of the store and down another and then stopped in front of the hair ribbons and bows. Even though she knew Jo might be surprised, Hailey picked out a bright red bow with sparkly fake diamonds on it. It was the most beautiful bow in the store.

Satisfied, she showed Mrs. Kirby her selections.

"Perfect," she said to her. "Lovely ideas."

Brimming with pleasure, Hailey handed the lady at checkout her money and put the gifts down.

"Somebody is going to have a nice Christmas," the lady said, smiling at her.

Hailey nodded. *My sisters.* Even thinking the word sister made Hailey's heart pound with excitement, and nervousness too. It was all so new.

At home, Hailey and Mrs. Kirby worked together wrapping the gifts in Mrs. Kirby's bedroom where they had privacy. The pretty green paper and shiny silver bows seemed like gifts of their own. Hailey did her best to make the paper not so crinkly and to stick the bow in exactly the right place.

Mrs. Kirby handed her the name tags. "Okay, now you need to add these. One for each of the girls. I've printed them carefully so you can read them."

Hailey proudly attached the name tags to the right gifts. She couldn't wait to see if the girls liked them.

She carefully carried them into the living room and placed them under the tree.

"Don't look, Charlie!" She hid the stuffed dog behind her back.

Mrs. Kirby smiled at her. "Tomorrow is going to be so much fun. Now let's see how the other girls are doing with icing the cookies they made earlier."

When they walked into the large kitchen, Alissa, Stevie, and Jo were standing around the kitchen island exclaiming over the cookies.

"Stevie's are the best," Jo said, and nobody disagreed. Hers were gorgeous, with a few extra touches on the Christmas trees and on Santa's face.

"Did you save a couple of cookies for Hailey to ice, like I asked?" Mrs. Kirby said.

Jo nodded. "Here, Hailey, these are yours."

Hailey swallowed hard. "Mine?"

"Yes. They're yours. Here's the icing and here is the spreader. Go to it," Jo said.

A few moments later, Hailey stood back. The green and red colors weren't exactly where she'd wanted them—they sort of blended too much—but the cookies were beautiful just the same.

"Go ahead and lick the spoon. We left some for you," said Mrs. Kirby.

The sugary taste on Hailey's tongue was delicious. "Mmm," she murmured, bringing a knowing smile to Mrs. Kirby's face.

Christmas morning, Alissa jumped out of bed. "Get up, sleepyhead! It's Christmas!"

Hailey's eyes flew open. It had just been moments ago that she lay awake wondering if Christmas was ever going to come. She scrambled out of bed and raced after Alissa.

Downstairs, Mrs. Kirby was in the living room with Jo and Stevie.

"Merry Christmas, girls! Come join us."

They sat together around the Christmas tree. Hailey stared at the number of brightly wrapped packages with awe. She'd never lived in a house where there were so many.

"Let's take turns opening gifts," said Mrs. Kirby.

Watching the girls open her presents for them, Hailey felt warm inside. They'd each liked her gift. She could tell. Stevie even understood why she'd chosen a notebook with a fox on it. Her last name was Fox.

And when she opened her own gifts, she almost squealed with delight. Colored pencils, pens, a notebook with a picture of a Dachshund on it, a drawing pad, and not one, but two books were hers. The notebook even had her name printed on it in big black letters.

Charlie, it's the best Christmas ever. Maybe there really is a Santa Claus.

She'd always remember this day—the music, the lights on the tree, the sound of crinkling paper, the cries of surprise. She studied Mrs. Kirby laughing with the other girls and felt as if she was in a dream.

Mrs. Kirby leaned over and gave her a kiss on the cheek. "We all have so much to be thankful for."

Yes, Charlie, you and me. Hailey hugged him hard, her eyes filling with tears of joy.

Hailey Kirby sat in the Granite Ridge, Idaho, library on a small wooden chair in the middle of a circle of wide-eyed three-to-six-year-old children sitting on the plush, new, green carpet in the children's section. Story time was her favorite activity of her job as assistant librarian and director of children's programs, and she loved to make it as exciting as possible by acting out the characters with different voices and mannerisms.

Though their town was small, the two-story, red-brick library building was an important part of the community. It had become a gathering place for various activities. Volunteer groups used the conference room for meetings, and the book club, which had started as a small group, had grown large enough to meet there every month, filling the largest room. Best of all, the library was a place that introduced the joys of reading to children.

As she leafed through the book she was reading

aloud, she studied the pictures carefully—pictures drawn by her own hand. That was something very few people knew. As part of her contract with a well-known children's book publisher, Hailey, writing and illustrating under the name of Lee Merriweather, had demanded anonymity. After lengthy discussions and with the help of her sister, Jo, acting as her lawyer, she finally won. She knew, though, as Lee Merriweather's popularity grew, she would eventually be exposed. Maybe by then, she'd be more comfortable about people knowing who she really was.

"What's Charlie going to do now?" asked one of the children, giving her a worried look.

"Is he going to get into trouble again?" another child asked.

Hailey held up a finger. "Let's see. Shall we?" One of the main characters in her stories was a boy named Charlie. He and his three friends found themselves in all kinds of trouble as they learned one life lesson after another. Each book had a happy ending, of course, because she understood how important they were.

Hailey read:

"Charlie's mother hugged him tight. 'I'm so glad you came home. I missed you.'

'I promise not to run away again,' said Charlie. He hadn't been gone long. After going only one block with his dachshund, Zeke, he wished he hadn't done it. Like his mother had told him, 'Home is where the heart is', and he knew his home was with her and the rest of his family."

"I'm glad Charlie went home," said a little girl named Regan, whom Hailey adored.

"Me, too," said Hailey. She'd found a home with Maddie Kirby when she was eight years old and would do anything in the world to repay her. It was one reason she'd come back to Granite Ridge after college. If Mom ever needed her, she'd be there in a heartbeat.

She helped the children replace their chairs at the tables set aside for them in the children's corner and checked her watch. She had just a few more hours until it was time for her to go home to pack for her stay with her family at the Cedar Mountain Lodge. She was both excited and saddened by the idea.

Alissa, her sister, had been dumped by her fiancé, Jed, days before their Christmas Eve wedding. Alissa told everyone in the family to go ahead with plans to spend time at the lodge. Travel arrangements had already been made for those flying in, the lodge had accommodations for them all, and her ex fiancé, the rat, could very well find other arrangements for the holiday. In an effort to cheer her and continue their family tradition of spending the holidays together, Hailey, her sisters, and their mom all agreed to keep to those plans. But Hailey ached for her sister. Jed had seemed the perfect man for her, and he'd disappointed them all.

Hailey spent time speaking to parents as they picked up their children from story time. She accepted hugs from all the children, loving the feel of their little arms around her.

When Nick Hensley entered the room, her pulse sputtered and kicked into a sprint. With his black, curly hair, brown eyes, and strong physique, he was beyond a hottie. The black ski jacket he wore stretched across his broad chest as if it had been made especially for him.

"Hi, Hailey. I'm here for Regan," Nick announced, looking around. "Where is she?" He sometimes helped his sister, Stacy, take care of Regan when she was too busy at the candy store in town to pick her up herself.

"Here! I'm here!" Laughing, Regan poked her head from behind a corner of the book shelf and ran to him, her arms open wide, her pink snow jacket flying behind her dark curls.

He swung her up in his arms and hugged her to him. "Okay, monkey, time to go to the store. Your mom is still working."

"Are you going to stay with us?" she asked.

He shook his head. "No, I have to go to work at the lodge. I make music there for everyone. Remember? Say thank you to Miss Kirby."

"Kisses! I want kisses," Regan said, reaching for Hailey, her brown eyes shining.

Hailey came close enough for Regan to kiss her.

Hailey closed her eyes as Regan planted a kiss on her cheek, wondering how it would feel if Nick did the same. She inhaled the smell of his lemony after-shave and sighed as he stepped away. They'd talked as friends about books, the weather and such, but that was as far as it went.

"Okay, then. Regan will see you next time," said Nick in his deep sexy voice. He started to leave and turned back to her. "I did as you suggested and wrote to Lee Merriweather. I got an email back from her stating she'd be happy to consider my creating a couple of children's songs to go with her books."

"How nice," she replied with a smile, trying not to give herself away. "I think it's a great idea."

Nick shook his head. "There's something about those stories of hers. They're special. Because Regan loves them so much, I swear I've read each book of hers about a hundred times, and every time I'm reminded of something in my own childhood. Weird, huh?"

"Maybe. But I'm sure it would make her happy to hear that." Hailey's heart sang. His kind words made all the hard work, all the long hours of writing and illustrating a children's book worthwhile.

"Well, I guess I'd better go." Still holding Regan in his arms, he walked out of the library.

Hailey sighed again. Lee Merriweather was more real to Nick than she was. Didn't he remember meeting her as a young girl? The sweet way he'd knelt down to say hi was something she'd never forget. She'd been crushing on Nick since she was a kid.

Back then, she'd been a lot shyer, a lot quieter.

Growing up, her thick eyeglasses and strawberry-blond hair that would never cooperate didn't help. Everyone in her family told her she was adorable, a little pixie, and though she loved them for it, she knew better. Just before she entered high school, they all surprised her with Lasik surgery. It was the sweetest, best gift she could've imagined, a chance to do without her hated glasses. At the time, she couldn't stop crying at their kindness. The memory still brought tears to her eyes.

In her books, Charlie, too, wore eyeglasses. No coincidence.

Karen Peterson, the head librarian, walked over to Hailey. "I'm so sorry about Alissa's broken engagement. She deserves much better treatment than that."

"Yes, I think so too. My family is going to go ahead with their plans to stay at the lodge through Christmas to New Year's Day. I think it'll be good for all of us."

"Such a sweet family you have, Hailey," Karen said, beaming at her. "Maddie was so lucky to find you four girls."

"No," Hailey said firmly. "We girls are the lucky ones." She'd loved going from somebody no one wanted to one of the Kirby girls.

"Well, enjoy yourselves. And when you come back, be ready to go to work. I'll have a hard time explaining to the little ones why their marvelous Miss Kirby is away. Thank goodness our volunteers are willing to step in to give you the time off."

"The volunteers are wonderful. I can't thank them enough." Living in a small town like Granite Ridge had its advantages. The idea of supporting one another was a part of it.

After Karen left, Hailey quickly wrote down instructions for the volunteers and mentioned a couple of books they might like to read aloud to the children. Every time she discovered a new book by a fellow author, she was thrilled to introduce it to the children. In some ways, it reminded her of her first night at her mother's house when she was a frightened little girl of eight. The story her mother read to her and Alissa was still one of her favorites. Who could resist saying goodnight to the moon?

With everything prepped at the library, Hailey bundled up, said goodbye to Karen, and headed out the door. Before going home to her condo, she had one errand to make. Hensley's Sweet Shoppe made the best chocolate-coated, caramel kisses ever. Those special holiday sweets were one of the first things her sisters asked for whenever they came home to visit. She planned to surprise them with a big box of the candy.

The frosty air outside took her breath away and nipped at her nose. But Hailey didn't mind. It was part of the charm of the season. Absorbing the bright colors of the lights and the holiday displays in the shop windows, she hurried along the street.

Hensley's Sweet Shoppe had a delightful, old-fashioned look to it with large paned-glass windows covering most of the front of the store on either side of the bright-red front door. The humidity of the indoor air had coated the windows with a frosty look that made the store even more inviting.

Hailey stepped inside, inhaled the enticing, sugary aroma, and grinned. Though she was careful about eating too many, she loved her sweets.

"Hey, Hailey! I've got your order for Christmas Kisses all ready for you," said Stacy, smiling at her, her hazel eyes agleam. She was all but hidden behind a starched, white apron. Her hair was covered by a pink baseball cap she wore to work in, but it couldn't hide a brown curl that trailed out from under it.

"Thanks!" said Hailey. "They're the best."

"By the way, I appreciate your including Regan in story time," Stacy said. "I know she's a little young to be there without me sitting with her, but it means the world to her to be able to be with the other kids to listen to you."

"No problem. I adore her. Regan is better behaved than some of the older kids, and she genuinely loves the stories. That means a lot."

"Regan and Nick both love to read." Stacy shook her head. "I swear, if Nick ever had the chance to meet the author of those Charlie books, he'd fall in love with her. He thinks she must be the most wonderful woman in the world."

"Really?" Hailey couldn't hold back her surprise.

Stacy nodded. "Oh, yeah. He hasn't told me too

much about his time away playing guitar in his band, but he's one disillusioned guy about women. Apparently, they fell all over him because of his fame and so-called fortune. After being cheated out of a lot of money by his agent and with Mom's death, Nick was more than ready to come back to Granite Ridge to help me. Nick and I have promised to honor Mom's wishes to keep the candy store going. Thank goodness because that lying, cheating, scumbag ex of mine left me high and dry."

Stacy, as chatty as her mother had been, continued. "Yeah, underneath all the glamour, Nick is a quiet man who loves music and is content sharing it with others in a whole new way at the lodge." She winked. "I can't believe Stevie's younger sister has grown into such a beauty. You were always so shy, so hidden behind those glasses of yours. But you were adorable, Hailey. I remember all too well how you and those dogs of yours followed your sisters and me around for a bit."

Hailey laughed. Another part of living in a small town meant your past was bound to nip you in the behind from time to time. "About the box of caramels?"

"Ah yes," said Stacy. "Here they are."

Hailey paid for the candy and waved goodbye. "Happy Holidays, Stacy. Give Regan a hug and a kiss for me."

"Will do. She's with the sitter, but I'll tell her. Best to all of you Kirbys."

A warm feeling kept the chill of the air away as

Hailey hurried back to the library to get her car. She gripped the box of candy kisses in her hand. Kisses both real and imagined had been part of her life as a Kirby since the time her new mother gave her a stuffed dog to help make her feel more comfortable in her new home. At the suggestion of one of her sisters, she'd named that little, soft dog Charlie Brown. Other, real dogs followed.

In time, Hailey hoped to have a family of her own, complete with dogs. But in order to make that happen, she needed to find the right man.

CHAPTER 2

H ailey stepped inside her condo, one of
several new ones built near the river. She
stood a moment, allowing her gaze to
sweep around the interior. Owning the condo was a
matter of pride for her. It represented years of hard
work studying for a degree, working at the library,
and establishing a business in the book industry with
the help of her clever sister, Jo, a lawyer who lived in
Chicago. With the sale of her first children's book she
had enough money for a down payment. Since then,
she'd been able to furnish it nicely. Living in the same
town as her mother made it perfect. Even though she
was grown, she relished the idea they could talk in
person over coffee or a cup of tea on a regular basis.
And if Mom were ever in trouble, she'd be right here
to help her.

One of the things she liked most about her condo
was the amount of natural light the plentiful
windows and a skylight provided. The second

bedroom was a perfect office and studio for her. She walked over to the sliding doors leading to the deck outside the living room. In the distance, the Cedar Mountain Lodge stood sentinel over the little town at the base of the mountain, giving the residents a sense of peace. As a major employer, the lodge was an important part of life year-round in Granite Ridge.

Staring at the lodge, she thought of what Stacy had told her about Nick. She'd wondered why he'd left the glamorous life of playing in a rock band, feeling there was something more than family obligations responsible. She was glad Nick hadn't fallen into the heady rock band scene, using girls and drugs as part of that life. It meant her impression of him while she was growing up was real.

She went into her bedroom to pack, and took a moment to assess herself. Lasik surgery had done wonders not only to her eyes but for her entire face. Gone were the hated glasses, exposing her large blue eyes and delicate features. With her strawberry-blond hair cut short and with wispy curls framing her face, it was no wonder she often had been chosen to play an angel in Christmas pageants.

She studied her body. Working out in the gym kept her in good shape. Though tiny, she had curves in all the right places. With three sisters, her fashion sense was kept up to date—fashion-forward and classic clothing served her well. The black wool slacks she wore fit her to a tee. The green, cashmere, cable-knit sweater she'd found on sale and the little

Christmas tree pin one of the children had given her last year added a nice holiday touch to her outfit.

She looked through her closet, searching for the right clothes to take with her. It would be cold on the mountain. Still, she would take a long, sleeveless gown to wear for the festive New Year's Eve celebration.

When at last she'd packed what she wanted, including a book or two to read if she had the chance, Hailey headed to her silver Honda SUV. She'd stop at Mom's house before heading up the mountain to make sure everything was set there.

As Hailey drew closer to the large, red-brick Victorian house, gratitude washed over her. And when the house came into view, she automatically smiled. She'd always thought her childhood home was beautiful with its white gingerbread trim, like icing on a favorite cake.

She checked the driveway. Neither Mom's car nor Alissa's rental was there. Pleased that plans were on schedule, Hailey kept driving. The empty driveway meant Mom was on her way to the airport to pick up Nan, the girls' grandmother, and Alissa had already left for the lodge.

The drive up to the Cedar Mountain Lodge was impressive with its twists and turns. Hailey studied her surroundings, following the road that led her through the tended forest. In a clearing near the top of the mountain, the lodge sat like royalty overlooking a kingdom. She never tired of seeing it. The main building's exterior was of polished logs and was flanked by two, three-story wings in brown brick that complemented the natural mountain character of the main lodge. She, like most year-round residents, knew that each of the wings held 72 rooms, for a total of 144 guest rooms. More guest rooms, including the Presidential Suite, were housed in the main building. The property also contained several small, private cabins.

She pulled up to the wide porte cochere and sat a moment admiring the sparkling white lights wound around the pillars holding it up. In the middle of the front circle of the hotel, a huge fir tree was decorated with more white lights and shimmering silver and gold ornaments.

"So pretty," murmured Hailey as a valet approached her door.

Hailey stepped outside the car and breathed in the crisp cool air with a new sense of peace. Staying here would be good for the entire family.

She walked into the front entry and immediately felt her gaze drawn into the lobby where a large Christmas tree stood beside the towering stone fireplace in the center of the room, open to both sides of the large space. The multi-colored lights and sparkling glass ornaments on the tree were reflected in the sliding glass doors that led to the wide patio outdoors.

Hailey smiled. It was as beautiful as she remembered. The lobby was decorated with greenery and candles everywhere, lending soft light and the smell of fresh evergreens to the entire area. The deep-red,

Oriental-style carpeting added another holiday touch.

"The Registration Desk is to your left," prompted a bellman who'd placed her luggage on a rolling cart.

"Thank you," Hailey said. She quickly texted Alissa to let her know she'd arrived.

Alissa promptly replied: *I'm in room 316.*

As soon as Hailey had her luggage situated in her suite, she hurried to Alissa's room.

When Alissa opened the door and saw Hailey, tears filled her eyes.

Hailey swept her sister into her arms. "How are you doing? I got here as soon as I could."

Alissa squeezed her hard and then stepped back. "I'm okay, I guess. It's so different from what I thought it'd be." Her breath caught. "I'm glad I'll have my family around to help me get through this mess."

"I'm here now, and the others are coming. We all support you, Alissa. We love you." Hailey drew in a deep breath, trying to calm the anger building inside her. "I'm so disappointed in Jed. I've always liked him. It makes me furious that he called off the wedding."

"Things just became so complicated and confusing between us. His mother ..." She trailed off and bowed her head. "I can't talk about it yet. Not even to you."

Alissa took hold of Hailey's arm and tugged her into the room. "I didn't mean to keep you standing there. Do you want anything to drink or eat? I could order something for you, if you want." Her lips trembled. "I can't eat or drink a thing."

Hailey glanced past the living area into the bedroom and saw the rumpled bedsheets.

"Were you sleeping?"

Alissa swept a lock of rich brown hair away from her face. "Yes, that seems the only way I can handle this. Not that I'm actually asleep. But letting my body rest while I'm trying to calm my mind seems to help."

Hailey was alarmed by the way Alissa's body was slumped with defeat. She was wearing a nightgown Hailey remembered from last Christmas. Nothing appropriate for a wedding week. Her heart ached for her sister.

"Is there anything I can do for you?"

Alissa shook her head. "Actually, I just need some time to myself."

"Okay, then," said Hailey. "Let me help you into bed and I'll leave. But, if you change your mind, I'm just a text away."

Hailey led Alissa like a child to the king-size bed and tucked her in.

Hailey bundled up and went outdoors for a walk. In the growing dark, Christmas lights twinkled at her, making it seem as if she'd stumbled into a fairyland.

Pulling her scarf tighter around her neck, she headed out to explore. The family was going to congregate for dinner a little later, but for now everyone was on her own.

The crunch of snow under her warm Ugg boots was a sound she liked. Her town below in the valley had a scattering of snow, but here, up in the mountains, the snow was deep and satisfying, especially for the skiers.

She walked to a separate log building and, hearing the sounds of music, opened the door and went inside the Granite Bar. A long wooden bar extended across one side wall with plenty of bar stools in front of it. A raised dais in the back of the rustic-decorated room held band instruments behind an empty dance floor. Music was coming from speakers mounted in strategic spots on the ceiling. People were sitting at the bar or at tables throughout the room filling the space with the happy sound of conversation and laughter.

Hailey stood a moment taking it all in and saw Nick standing by the side of the stage surrounded by a group of women. He noticed her and waved her forward.

Surprised but pleased, she moved through the crowd toward him and the group around him.

As she neared them, he called out to her, "Hi, sweetheart!"

She stopped and swiveled to see who must be behind her. He never called her anything but Hailey or Miss Kirby.

Nick walked over to her, flung an arm around her

shoulder, and murmured into her ear, "Just play along with me. OK?"

She nodded, too startled to comment.

The five women who'd been talking to him glared at her. As they walked by, one of them boldly wiggled her fingers at Nick. "Like I said, anytime, Nick."

Nick continued to keep his arm around Hailey until the last of the group had merged into the revelers. "Thanks for helping me out," he said, taking a step back. "Some fans are willing to do anything to be with a band member. In the beginning, I thought it was cool. Now, I know better."

Hailey studied him. Whether he was in a band or not, he was one gorgeous hunk of male. Her heart was still racing from being so close to him.

"Guess you're here for Alissa's wedding," he said.

"Her non-existent wedding," said Hailey, making a face. "We're all so disappointed."

"If there's anything I can do for you, let me know. I can hook up some special music for you, or whatever."

"Thanks. That's very nice of you," said Hailey, touched by his concern. "Well, I guess I'd better go."

"Come back tonight. I'll be here. I owe you at least one dance." His grin lit his dark eyes. As she found herself falling into their depth, she felt a tug of desire. *Whoa!*

"Maybe," she replied, hoping he wasn't aware of his effect on her. She was here for her sister's non-wedding, not for some hot time with the sexiest guy she'd ever known.

She was still shaken by the experience as she left the bar and walked along the path past the tiny village of stores over to where several private honeymoon cabins were tucked into the woods. Observing how cute they were, Hailey's heart clenched. *Poor Alissa!*

She thought back to her childhood. She and Alissa had shared a room for years. Like any two girls living in close quarters, they'd had a few spats, but nothing like regular sisters. They were, after all, soul sisters with a deeper connection between them than most siblings.

By the time Hailey returned to her hotel room, she was ready to meet up with her other siblings. Spending every holiday season together was a wonderful way to help keep the family strong.

She hung up her coat, grabbed the box of candy, and hurried to Alissa's room, anxious to see her sisters. They were gathered in Alissa's suite in a show of support. They planned to have dinner in one of the hotel's restaurants afterwards. For now, it was time to catch up with everyone.

Entering the room and placing the box of candy on a coffee table in the living area, Hailey cried, "Christmas Kisses!"

Alissa and Stevie raced to the box.

"Yum!" cried Stevie. "I always know I'm home for the holidays when these appear."

Hailey embraced her. Red-haired, freckled-face

Stevie was a free spirit who always brought a sense of fun to any occasion. Hailey loved being with her.

She'd see Jo at dinner. Her oldest sister was smart as a whip, super independent, and very protective of her sisters. She'd been a whiz at negotiating the book contract for her. Hailey would always be grateful to her.

Mom would be along later with Nan, but she loved it when all her girls got together.

CHAPTER 3

After they finished dinner in the main dining room, Hailey stood with her sisters.

"Anyone interested in going to the Granite Bar?" Now that Nick had asked her to come, she wanted to see if what she'd imagined between them was the least bit real.

"Maybe later," said Jo. "I want to spend some time with Mom."

"Me, too," Alissa said. "But, go, Hailey. It will do you good to get out and about."

"I'll go with you," said Stevie. "I'll meet you in the lobby in ten minutes."

Hailey got her coat and went down to the lobby. Stevie promptly showed up, and together, they walked through the snowy night to the Granite Bar.

"Are you dating anyone?" Hailey asked her.

"Not at the moment," Stevie said. "How about you?"

Hailey shook her head. "Not for a while now. I just haven't found anyone who really interests me."

Stevie placed a hand on her shoulder. "No worries. It'll happen." The smile fell from her face. "Although, considering what Alissa's going through, embracing single life seems way smarter."

"But lonelier."

Stevie shot Hailey a look. "Yeah, maybe," she admitted grudgingly.

When they walked through the door of the bar, Hailey glanced around, but saw no sign of Nick.

"Over here," said Stevie, grabbing hold of her elbow and leading her to one of two empty bar stools.

The bartender, a pretty girl with a broad smile, said, "What'll you have?"

Hailey ordered an IPA.

Stevie asked for a Moscow Mule with extra lime, then leaned against the counter and looked around. "A pretty cool place. Looks like an interesting crowd." She smiled as a young man approached. "Oh my gosh! Is that you Nicky?"

Nick grinned. "Yeah, it's me. I'm here to make sure I get a dance with your sister. I owe her one."

Stevie's eyebrows shot up. She gave Hailey a sly look. "Okay then, sis. Off you go."

Hailey tried to act nonchalant as she accepted Nick's hand and dismounted from the stool, but her pulse was racing. She fought a stumble and quickly righted herself.

Nick and she wended their way through the crowd to the dance floor. The loud music dimmed and ended, then a slow number came on.

"When does the band start playing?" Hailey asked, desperate to find conversation. She'd be darned if she'd talk about the weather.

Nick checked his watch. "In about a half-hour. Be sure to stick around. They're good. Just here for one night." He moved her smoothly across the dance floor away from the cluster of people in the middle.

"Thanks again for helping me. And by the way, thanks for being so good with Regan. That means a lot to Stacy and me."

"She's darling. I really enjoy her."

"Do you have any ideas for the songs I want to write about Lee Merriweather's books? You seem to know her work so well."

"Something simple for children, maybe with a little syncopation so the songs are fun and off beat. And always something about friends and family."

He gazed down at her. "You sound just like the author. I like that about you."

Hailey smiled, unwilling to let him know the truth. She wanted people to like her for herself.

When the music stopped, they faced one another.

"Thanks for the dance," said Hailey, sorry it was over. In his arms, she felt as if she'd found a different kind of home.

He studied her, his features softening. "If you're still here and I can break free, let's do it again."

"Okay," Hailey said. "I don't know how late I'll stay."

He winked at her. "There's always tomorrow."

She laughed with pleasure and headed back to Stevie.

"Wow!" Stevie said. "You guys really have chemistry, hey?"

"What do you mean? He just asked me to thank me for something I did earlier."

"Oh?" asked Stevie, arching an eyebrow. "That was pretty up close and personal for a '*thank-you*,'" she said making air quotes with her hands.

Hailey gave her sister a playful push. "Don't worry. He's a nice guy, but he has women falling all over him all the time. He's not really interested in me."

As she acknowledged the fact, her heart skipped a beat and seemed to fall to her feet. That's all this was about. A dance, a thank you, not the beginning of a romance. She'd been foolish to think for a moment it was anything more.

Stevie sighed gustily and stretched. "Whew, too much sitting for this girl today. I've got to stretch my legs, go for a walk or something. Are you ready to head out?"

Hailey darted a glance toward Nick and to her chagrin, Stevie caught the look and chuckled. "Oh, I see how it is. You want to stay, and you should. I think he really likes you too. Do you mind if I take off though?"

"No, no. Go ahead. I won't be late," Hailey said, reassuring her.

Hailey watched her sister leave, and after waiting awhile and realizing Nick was still busy with his work, she prepared to leave.

A voice from the crowd behind her said, "Hailey? Is that you?"

Hailey turned around to see a heavy-set woman with frosted blond hair striding toward her with a big smile. She jumped to her feet. "Casey Richards! What are you doing here?"

Laughing, they embraced. "My boyfriend and I thought it would be fun to spend the holidays in ski country. He's a big skier. Me? Not so much. How about you?"

"I'm here with my family to celebrate my sister's wedding, only there isn't one. Her fiancé, the jerk, called it off a couple of days ago."

"Oh, gosh! I'm sorry to hear that." Casey rubbed her hands together and gave Hailey a teasing grin. "Maybe that's a case for Lulu Rocket."

Hailey chuckled. Lulu Rocket was a fictional character in a middle-grade fantasy book series of Casey's and was always called upon to save a situation. Hailey had met Casey at a writer's conference and had been drawn to her and her characters from the beginning. Lulu and her friends always brought justice to the world.

"Right now, my sister, Alissa, is devastated, but she's strong. We're all here to give her support."

"I'm going to have a lot of free time with Eric

skiing all day. Want to get together to enjoy some of the other activities around here?"

Hailey smiled and nodded. "That would be great. Alissa said she needs some time alone, and though I want to give her all the space she needs, I want to try everything here."

Casey gave her a high-five. "Sounds hunky-dory."

Hailey laughed. Lulu Rocket used that word a lot.

A stocky, blond-haired man approached. Casey turned to him with a smile. "Meet Hailey Kirby, or perhaps I should say, Lee Merriweather, a writing friend of mine. She and her family are here. Hailey, this is Eric Olsen."

Hailey returned Eric's smile and shook his hand.

"Aren't you the one Casey told me about who writes the Charlie books?" he asked.

"Yes," said Hailey. "Nice to meet you."

"Same here." He turned to Casey. "I'm about ready to head up to our room."

"Me, too." Casey hugged her. "I'm so glad we met up. I'll call you in the morning. I'm thinking of going to the cookie decorating party."

"Sounds good."

As they walked out the door leaving Hailey alone, Nick came up to her. "Sorry we didn't get a chance for another dance. I was looking forward to it."

"Maybe another time," said Hailey. At the thought, a thread of excitement wove through her.

They gazed at one another and then Nick was

called away. As he returned to the stage area, a woman who'd been in the group surrounding him earlier got up from a nearby table and followed him.

Reminded once more about the danger of falling for a guy like that, Hailey left the bar.

CHAPTER 4

After a restless night in which Hailey dreamed of dancing with Nick, she lay on her back staring up at the ceiling feeling glum. She'd definitely felt a connection to him, but any kindness he'd shown her was just that, kindness. And he'd been clear about not wanting attention from the women in the room.

Her cell phone rang. *Mom.*

"Hi, Mom. What's up?"

"We're all meeting for breakfast at the café by the lobby. And I thought it would be nice if as many of us who could went to the cookie decorating party the hotel is putting on for guests this morning. We didn't have a chance to do our usual baking at home, and Alissa mentioned it might be fun."

"I've just ordered room service." Just saying it made Hailey want to curl her toes with pleasure. She'd saved a long time for this holiday vacation and wanted to enjoy every minute she could and still support Alissa.

"That sounds lovely, but afterwards, please stop by the café to see us," said Mom. "I'm glad you're finally getting some time to relax. Between your job and your books, you seem to have little time for fun."

"I know," Hailey admitted. People might not understand her need to write these stories. In some ways writing them was therapeutic. Before she'd come to Maddie Kirby's home, her life had been difficult, to say the least. She loved being able to create characters to whom children and adults could relate and delighted in giving them happy endings like hers.

"Enjoy your breakfast," said Mom. "I'll see you later in the cafe."

"Okay," Hailey said, clicking off the call. She'd just have time for a nice hot shower before her breakfast was due to arrive.

Later, as she dressed for the day in jeans and a warm, fuzzy blue sweater that matched her eyes, Hailey decided not to worry about Nick Hensley. The whole idea of anything happening between them was ludicrous. He was a nice guy. But after traveling the world with his music, why would he settle for small town life in Granite Ridge? After a year or two, he was bound to get bored. And she'd never leave town; she was dedicated to her family.

A knock on the door sounded. Stomach growling with hunger, she raced to answer it.

A member of the room service staff smiled at her and rolled in a serving cart with her breakfast.

Feeling very sophisticated, Hailey stood aside while the young man set up her breakfast on a table in the living area of her suite.

"Anything else?" he asked when he was finished.

"No, thank you. This is perfect." She couldn't stop smiling.

The waiter left, and Hailey sat down to enjoy her breakfast. Gazing out the window, she delighted in the view of snow-covered evergreens, the distant peaks of the mountains, and the sun shimmering on the ice crystals atop the snow, making the landscape sparkle and glow. Farther down the hill, she saw the ice-skating rink and decided to do some skating while she was here.

She was halfway through her breakfast when another knock came at the door.

Hailey set down her fork and hurried to answer it. "Alissa! Hi! How are you doing?" She hugged her hard. "Come on in. Have you eaten yet?"

Alissa shook her head. "I'm not hungry."

"Oh, hon," said Hailey. "Come sit. You need something. You may have my pastry, and I'll fix a cup of coffee for you."

Alissa allowed Hailey to lead her to the table.

Hailey poured fresh coffee into one of the mugs provided in the suite and set a plate with a pastry in front of Alissa.

"I'm sorry to see you so unhappy, Alissa. You know I'd do anything to take the hurt away."

Alissa nodded and looked up at Hailey with watery eyes. "I know. I just can't believe what happened. I know what Jed and I shared was true love."

Thinking of Nick and the feelings he'd aroused in her, Hailey sat and studied her. "How do you know if it's true love, Alissa? I've dated men but never had the feeling that I couldn't live without any of them. Maybe I didn't give them a real chance. Is there something wrong with me?"

"No, Hailey. You just haven't met the right man yet. When you do, believe me, you'll know." A faraway look crossed Alissa's face. "I knew right away Jed was the one for me."

Hailey was quiet. She recalled the way she'd felt in Nick's arms and the desire that had filled her. Then she remembered her earlier thoughts about him being unhappy after living a while in Granite Ridge.

Alissa gave her a teasing smile. "Why are you asking? Are you talking about Nick Hensley? Stevie told me about the two of you dancing together last night."

Hailey couldn't hide the way her cheeks heated. "Well, it's not quite that way. He just was thanking me for helping him out earlier. That's all."

Alissa laughed. "Hailey, you never could hide your feelings."

"Oh, all right. I think he's nice and hot and … and … everything. But I don't want to get hurt like you. Look at him! He's gorgeous, and he can have anyone he wants."

Alissa shook her head. "You've never really believed how beautiful you are—inside and out. If you think he might be the one, relax and find time to be together, and see how real it is."

She was right, Hailey thought. If given a chance to spend more time with Nick, she'd take it.

Later, as she spread green icing over the last of the Christmas tree cookies she'd chosen, a conversation at the other table in the room caught Hailey's attention.

"She's meeting up with Nick sometime today," said one of the girls she'd seen in the bar last night, "I swear, she's not going to give up until she gets him locked down. You know how she is."

The laughter from the other girls in the group made Hailey's stomach fill with acid.

Standing next to her, Casey elbowed her. "Hey, are you all right? You looked so sad. Is it your sister?"

"Yes," Hailey lied. Good thing to know that Nick wasn't entirely immune to advances by women. She'd almost made a mistake believing Nick might have some real interest in her. She glanced at Jo and Stevie working at the far end of the table. They were a lot wiser than she. Neither one had a boyfriend. And look at what had happened to Alissa. She'd just left, looking as sad as Hailey had ever seen her.

"Let's go ice skating," said Casey. "The sun is out

and it's a perfect time to do it. I need to work off the cookies I ate."

"Me, too," said Hailey. Thinking of Nick meeting another girl was something she'd have to try to forget.

Hailey and Casey walked down to the skating rink. It sat on the hillside below the hotel in a clearing that gave a sense of privacy to the skaters. This same area was used in the summer months as a venue for small concerts.

As they walked, they talked about the publishing business. Hailey told Casey about Nick's wish to write songs for her books. "He has no idea Lee Merriweather is me, and that's the way I want to keep it."

"Okay, though it might be a good idea if he did know. Then the two of you could really collaborate."

"He's asked for my ideas, and I'm willing to help him with that. But it's best if I don't get too involved."

Casey gave her a piercing look. "With him, you mean."

"Well, yes. Those girls were talking about Nick meeting up with one of them." Even saying the words stung.

"Hold on!" said Casey. "You can't judge him by someone else's words. Especially theirs. I saw them in action at the bar last night and the words sleazy and desperate come to mind."

Hailey waved away Casey's concern. "I know you're right, but I'll still keep my distance. Now, let's go get on that ice."

Casey grinned. "Sounds good to me."

They headed into the wooden building called The Skate Shack to check out skates. Socks, hats, mittens, and other sportswear with the lodge name and logo were for sale. A number of skaters sat on benches in front of a roaring fire in the massive stone fireplace along one outside wall. Cocoa, coffee, tea, and soft drinks were available for sale, along with cookies and donuts.

Hailey found a pair of skates small enough for her feet and eagerly sat down to put them on. Living in Granite Ridge with availability to the lodge, she'd skated before, of course. But she still enjoyed the thrill of lacing up skates to spend time circling on the ice.

Casey and she went out onto the rink. Trying to get into the rhythm of a freestyle pace, Hailey moved swiftly across the smooth ice the hotel maintained. Laughing for the pure pleasure of it, she went faster and faster.

A small child on ice skates darted in front of her.

Hailey tried to stop, swung out away from the child, and bumped into the back of a skater ahead of her.

"Whoa!" came a deep voice, and Nick turned around to face her. "Hey, Hailey! Guess that's one way to say hello." He gripped her arms to steady her.

"I'm sorry. I was trying to avoid running over a child in front of me." She looked up into his eyes and swore the temperature outdoors rose ten degrees.

Flustered by her thoughts, she pulled away from him. "What are you doing here? No work?"

"Things are pretty calm for the moment. I try to stay in shape for hockey. The guys in the area have formed a couple of teams and we play each other. I'm back on the job this evening. Say, do you have time this afternoon to discuss song ideas?"

"I don't think so. My friend Casey is here with her boyfriend, and we're spending time together while he's skiing."

"Oh, okay. Maybe later."

He seemed disappointed, but Hailey told herself not to care. More than ever, she knew what a threat he was with those dark eyes that reached deep inside her, making her wish for the impossible.

As soon as he skated away from her, another guy met up with him, and after talking a while, they both left the ice.

"You brush him off?" Casey asked her.

Hailey shrugged. "He just wanted to talk about the songs for my books."

"Yeah, I'm sure you're right," said Casey with enough sarcasm in her voice to make Hailey snicker.

Suddenly they were both laughing.

"Ah, Hailey, you're so much fun," said Casey, taking her elbow and skating around the rink with her.

CHAPTER 5

Hailey checked her watch, two o'clock. Snow was falling outside the restaurant near the skating rink where she and Casey were finishing lunch.

"This is a perfect afternoon for reading," Hailey announced. "I think I'll check in with family and then curl up with a book."

Casey nodded. "Okay. I'm going to do some work and then meet up with Eric. Promise me you'll join us for a late dinner at the Granite Bar. Their food is delicious, and all the skiers will be back and ready to party. I'll make the reservations."

Hailey hesitated and then agreed. She was here to have a good time, meet new people, and most of all, support her sister. She knew from an earlier conversation, Alissa had plans for the evening, and being with Casey was fun.

She walked outside, said goodbye to Casey, and lifted her face to the falling snow. With the fresh snow, the sky had turned a steel-gray making it easy to study the flakes falling toward her. Hailey stuck out her tongue to catch a few.

"Cute picture," said a deep-voice, snapping her to attention.

Hailey narrowed her eyes. "What are you doing here? Are you following me?"

Nick chuckled and shook his head. "Just checking on the audio equipment at the restaurant." He approached and carefully removed a snowflake clinging to one of her eyelashes. "You caught one."

She reached up and wiped the leftover moisture from her eyelid. "They're so beautiful falling from the sky like this. I love the idea that no two are exactly alike. Like all of us."

He smiled. "That's what Charlie says in one of his books."

"I imagine it's something that a lot of us think," she said, trying not to give herself away.

Nick nodded and studied her. "I know I've said this before, but I like you, Hailey. I want to get to know you better. Be sure to come to the Granite Bar tonight. I'll be playing with the band."

Hailey couldn't hide her surprise. "The band? Stacy told me you weren't playing with the band, that you wanted to be here in Granite Ridge."

Nick shrugged. "I can't just give up music. I formed a local band of guys who all live here. We have a contract to play at the lodge from time to time when I can schedule it in around my job working with the sound systems and other maintenance at the lodge. Believe me, I have no desire to go on the road again. That's why I decided to turn to songwriting, including songs for kids."

"Oh."

"And that's why I need your input on the ideas I have for Charlie Songs as I call them. I can't think of anyone else who might better understand what I'm trying to do because you read those books all the time."

"I see. Well, in that case, I'll find some time to help you. It's such a sweet idea."

"Lee Merriweather thought so too," he said, beaming at her. "How about tomorrow afternoon? I live in one of the cabins set aside for staff. I have my keyboard and music there. I'll even serve lunch."

Hailey drew in a deep breath.

Nick grinned. "Don't worry, you'll be safe with me."

"Okay," said Hailey, wondering if being safe is what she really wanted from him.

"Great. Gotta go. See you tonight," said Nick. He gave her a wave and, humming a song, disappeared into the restaurant.

Hailey returned to the hotel, her cheeks tingling from the cold. Still chilled from her walk from the restaurant, she hurried up to her room.

She checked her phone for any messages from the family and seeing none, kicked off her boots and jacket, grabbed a book, and headed into the bedroom. It pleased her to have this special time to herself. As a librarian and author, spending time like this was a precious gift.

She pulled back the duvet on her bed and climbed in under it. Soon she was lost in the book, and later, she fell asleep.

The chimes on her phone woke her.

She checked caller ID. *Casey.*

"Hi, what's up?" Hailey asked sleepily.

"I've got a date for you for tonight. I hope you don't mind, but a friend of Eric's is at the hotel, and we've asked him to join us for dinner. He's a real nice guy. I think you're going to like him. His name is Roger Evans. If I weren't already with Eric, I'd go for him."

Hailey hesitated for only a few seconds. "It sounds good."

"Great. Reservations are for eight o'clock. See you then." Casey clicked off the call.

Hailey stretched and checked the clock on the bedside table. Six o'clock. She'd have two hours to look good for Roger, she told herself, refusing to admit it was Nick she wanted to impress.

At quarter of eight, Hailey stood in front of the mirror giving herself a look of approval. Her black jeans fit her well and looked good tucked into the black cowboy boots she'd splurged on a few years ago. Her red turtleneck top popped with color beneath the black suede, fringed jacket she wore for warmth. It was a western look that suited her trim body and would fit right into the rustic décor of the bar.

Before leaving, she checked her phone for messages and found one she'd missed from Alissa saying she was going to have a quiet evening and would see her in the morning. Hailey already knew the rest of the family had plans of their own.

She left her room and took the elevator down to the lobby, mentally humming the Christmas carol that had been playing through the speakers. It made her think of Nick and all the work he did at the hotel to make sure appropriate music was played throughout the property.

As she stepped out of the elevator, Hailey studied the scene in the lobby. The Christmas tree and other decorations made the room come alive with color. The holiday outfits on the guests relaxing in comfortable chairs and on leather couches strategically placed throughout the room added to the festive décor.

Full of good cheer, Hailey headed to the Granite Bar for dinner.

The bar was crowded when she walked inside. She glanced around for Casey and found her sitting with Eric and another man in the back corner of the room near the stage. Overcome with apprehension, she paused then marched forward with determination. She wasn't the shy, little girl who was uncomfortable in a crowd meeting new people. She was Lee

Merriweather, successful author of stories about a little boy who wasn't afraid to try new things.

Eric stood with the other man. "Hi, Hailey. This is my friend, Roger Evans. Roger, meet Hailey Kirby."

A man not quite as tall as Eric but every bit as blond, smiled and shook her hand, his blue eyes alight with pleasure. "Glad you could join us for dinner."

He held a chair for her.

"Thank you," said Hailey, taking a seat, pleased by his manners.

"You look great, Hailey," said Casey. "I told Roger I thought you two might get along. I see it's already happening."

Hailey and Roger exchanged smiles. It felt good to be accepted so easily into the group.

Conversation among the four was easy. In addition to being skiers, Eric and Roger were friends from work at a communications company in Seattle. They talked about their day and plans to hit the slopes tomorrow, and then Casey told them about the fun she and Hailey had shared.

After they ordered their meals, Roger asked Hailey what she did for a living. She proudly filled him in on her work at the library and the reasons she'd come back to Granite Ridge.

Roger shook his head. "I was born in Seattle and couldn't think of leaving it." He chuckled. "Except to go skiing in the winter or to hit the islands for some sunshine."

"Islands?"

"In the Caribbean. I like to travel."

Hailey smiled, but she already knew as nice as he was, Roger was not for her.

She finished her burger and sipped her beer, relaxing with the others, waiting for the band to come on.

Nick approached their table. "Hi, Hailey. Glad you're here."

Hailey introduced him to the others, trying not to stare at the way his jeans hugged his body or the black T-shirt he wore that sculpted all the muscles in his arms and couldn't hide the shape of his ripped abs.

Casey said, "Have a seat. The band doesn't start until ten. Right?"

Nick nodded. "Saw you with Hailey at the rink today. Have fun?"

"Oh, yes," said Casey. "Tomorrow morning, we're going to try snowshoes. Right, Hailey?"

"Yes. We thought that would be fun."

Casey beamed at her. "And then in the afternoon …

"In the afternoon, I'm busy," said Hailey, making sure she didn't look at Nick.

"Yeah, she's going to help me with music. I'm writing some songs for Lee Merriweather's books."

"Isn't Hailey … OUCH!" cried Eric, leaning over and rubbing his leg.

"Hailey loves those books. I do too," said Casey. "Roger, tell us about your latest trip." She turned to Nick. "Roger likes to travel."

Hailey silently thanked Casey for the diversion. She wasn't ready to tell Nick who she was. She wasn't sure what his reaction would be when he discovered she was the woman his sister had said he'd probably fall in love with. That was just talk. If he was interested in her, she wanted it to be for herself.

She barely listened to Roger talk about his trip to the Canadian Rockies. Her mind was on Nick and the easy way he fit into the group.

A young woman came over to their table. "You're Nick Hensley, aren't you? Would you do me a favor and sign an autograph for my sister. She'll die when she hears I saw you."

Nick dutifully took the pen from her and the blank sheet of paper she handed him. "What's your sister's name? I'll sign it for her."

"You'd do that? Thank you so much! Her name is Lila. She's only fourteen, but she's a big fan of yours. Or was, until the band broke up."

"No problem." Nick scrawled a note on the paper and handed it back to the woman. "If you and she come back to the resort, I'd be glad to meet her."

The woman smiled at him. "You're a very nice man."

Hailey was amused by the color that crept into Nick's cheeks. Yeah, he wasn't the tough guy he appeared on the stage. Like Stacy said, he was really a quiet kind of man who liked to read to his niece and help out his family. If she wasn't already falling in love with him, after a moment like this, she would be.

"That was good, Nick," said Casey, echoing Hailey's thoughts.

He shrugged. "I'm just a guy who plays and writes music. Right now, I'd better go back and check the equipment here and also in the events building. I'll be back to play in a while."

After he left, Casey turned to her. "I'm going to the ladies' room. Care to join me?"

Hailey smiled and nodded, then rose with Casey.

Casey took her elbow and hustled her along to the ladies' room, which was surprisingly empty.

"Hailey Kirby, why didn't you tell me you loved Nick? As soon as he sat at the table, it was written all over your face."

Hailey's eyes widened. "Oh, no! Do you think he noticed?"

Casey shook her head. "No, I don't. While you were trying not to give yourself away, he was too busy mooning over you. I'm telling you right now, this is a love story in the making, or else I'm deaf and blind."

Hailey swallowed hard. Things were happening so fast. "Casey, you can't let on to Eric or anyone else. It's true that I'm attracted to Nick. Who wouldn't be? He's so nice, so talented, so sweet, so … hot."

Casey gave her a smug smile. "Yep, I knew it."

"Listen, it's important that he doesn't know that I'm Lee. Thank you for distracting Eric. If anything is to come of this, it has to be on my terms as Hailey, not the author his sister told me Nick was half in love with."

"Whoa! She told you that?"

"Yes, but it was just talk. She's a chatterbox."

"Oh, boy! Mark my words, you guys aren't going to make it to New Year's before you're a couple."

"Are you talking about going to bed together?" Hailey asked, both shocked and titillated by the idea.

"That's up in the air. I'm talking about the two of you admitting your love for one another."

"I don't know …"

Casey smiled. "I do. Sweet friend, you're about to go on the kind of journey our romance author friends describe. I just know it."

At the possibility, every nerve ending in Hailey came alive. Was this the beginning of the true love Alissa talked about?

When they returned to the table, some of the band members were on stage tuning instruments and making sure everything was ready for their performance. Hailey noted the lights that had come on in a banner above the stage. It read Granite Rock Band. From what she could see, there was a keyboard player, a drummer, and what looked like two guitarists, Nick and another man.

Several young women, bold from alcohol no doubt, approached the stage. "Where's Nick?" asked one of them.

"He's coming," said one of the musicians.

When Nick arrived, three women rushed toward him.

He chatted with them as he tuned his guitar and moved one of the microphones around.

Hailey watched with fascination as one of the women tried to climb onto the stage. Nick's sister had told her that he was tired of that kind of thing. She understood why.

Casey glanced from the group of women to her and shook her head. "Pathetic."

Sounds from the keyboard, accompanied by drums, chased the women away. Nick walked over to one of the standing microphones. "Good evening, ladies and gentlemen."

The sound in the bar became quieter.

"I'd like to introduce the Granite Rock Band. On drums, we have Richie Duncan, Mike Greenley on keyboard, Chico Alvarez on bass guitar, and me, Nick Hensley."

Members of the audience clapped or whistled or stamped their feet. Hailey smiled. It was going to be a good night.

Lights in the bar dimmed and colored lights washed over the stage from spotlights in the ceiling. The music began, and the whole room seemed to rock in time to the pounding beat. Nick did riffs on his guitar, his fingers flying up and down the neck of his guitar while the fingers of his other hand plucked at the strings so quickly they blurred. It was, thought Hailey, electrifying.

People stood and swayed to the music. She came to her feet and moved as one with the crowd, matching the rhythm.

When the song ended, she clapped and laughed for the pure joy of it. No wonder girls hung around the stage to get the attention of the members of the band. For as long as the song lasted, they were magical, forcing you to go along with them on their musical journey.

Casey pulled Hailey into a quick hug. "You're so fun to watch dance. No one would ever believe you're a librarian."

Hailey giggled. "Marian the librarian?"

"Something like that," said Casey laughing.

After a few more songs, Hailey was ready to go home. When Casey, Eric, and Roger got ready to leave, Hailey rose and waved goodbye to Nick.

His eyes bore into hers as he continued to play.

Hailey lifted a hand to her cheek. His sexy gaze had felt like a kiss.

CHAPTER 6

The next morning, Hailey and Casey stood with three other adults and an instructor going over the steps of learning to use snowshoes. They'd all been fitted with snowshoes and protective coverings over their boots. In addition, they'd been given two adjustable poles.

Following instructions, Hailey moved forward across the flat area that had been designated as a training ground. Later, they'd go into the woods to learn how to traverse rougher territory.

After an hour of trekking a trail in an area set aside for hikers with snowshoes, Casey turned to Hailey. "I don't know about you, but I'm ready to go sit and soak in one of the hot pools." Behind each wing of the hotel a large, round, heated shallow pool offered a spa-like rest to skiers and other guests.

"Sounds delightful," said Hailey, wiping a gloved hand across her flushed face. "This is a lot harder than it looks. My legs feel like wet noodles."

They thanked the instructor, handed in their gear, and headed back to the hotel to get changed. Hailey could hardly wait to sit and soak.

In her room, Hailey plugged in her phone to charge it. After changing into a bathing suit, she wrapped herself in the thick terrycloth robe that had been placed in her suite, slipped on shoes, and headed out to the east wing pool. She'd meet Casey there.

In the cool outdoors, she hurried to the warmth of the pool, disrobed, and climbed into the hot water. She gasped as she got accustomed to the heat and settled in. The sun shone in the bright sky above her, coating the surface of the water with a golden glow.

Hailey lay her head back against the edge of the pool and stared up at the sky, thinking of her reaction to Nick Hensley. She was as eager to be with him as the women who hung around the stage vying for his attention. She couldn't hide from it any longer. She was drawn to him in a way she'd never felt for any other man.

"Ah, it must feel good. You're smiling," said Casey, slipping into the water beside her.

"Aside from the disappointment for Alissa, this getaway is just what I needed. Everyone in the family is doing their own thing and getting together at different times, so it really feels like both a private and family vacation." Hailey turned to Casey with a smile. "I'm really glad I bumped into you. It's been fun to catch up."

"Thanks. Do you want to do lunch after this?"

Hailey shook her head. "No, thanks. That's part of the deal with my helping Nick. He's giving me lunch."

"Aha!" Casey elbowed her. "Sounds like you're really going to make music together."

Hailey laughed. "It's not like that."

"Right. I keep forgetting," Casey said, rolling her eyes.

The sexy thoughts of him that filled Hailey's mind abruptly ended when reality struck. Nick might say he wants to live a quiet life in Granite Ridge, but after seeing him in action, she found it difficult to believe. He was a natural on stage.

Later, giving herself just five minutes to get out the door and to his cabin, she grabbed her warm coat and headed out. Nick had texted her directions to his cabin and she'd memorized the way.

She was almost to Nick's cabin when she realized she didn't have her phone. She thought about going back for it and decided not to bother. This was vacation time.

As she approached the cabin, she heard the sound of music from within it. She knocked and waited for him to answer.

He opened the door and grinned at her. "Thanks for coming. I appreciate it."

Curious, she stepped inside. Aside from a jacket thrown across the couch and a few dishes on the kitchen counter, the place was tidy. A music keyboard and stool filled one corner of the room, not far from the stone fireplace.

"Here, let me take your coat," said Nick, politely standing by.

She shrugged out of it.

He took it and threw it on the couch.

She looked at him with surprise and then they both laughed.

"Guess I could've hung it up," he said. "C'mon. I had the chef in the hotel kitchen fix lunch for us. Hot soup and sandwiches."

She walked into the tiny kitchen and took a seat at the small, round wooden table for two. "It smells good."

"His famous vegetable soup and my favorite grilled cheese sandwiches," Nick said, pouring soup into two bowls.

He placed one of the bowls of soup, a napkin, and a spoon in front of her and did the same for himself before putting a plate of sandwiches in the middle of the table.

"I take it this is where you normally live when you're not staying in town," said Hailey.

"Yes. As long as I'm employed full-time and am on call for hotel maintenance emergencies, these are the living quarters the hotel gives me."

"Does it ever seem lonely?" she asked. "You're tucked way back into the woods."

"No, I don't mind being alone. And I'm not that

far away from a whole beehive of activity." He studied her. "Are you having a good vacation?"

She nodded and set down her soup spoon. "Except for the unhappiness I feel for Alissa, this has been great. I'm so busy with work I sometimes forget to stop and have fun."

"Work with the library?"

"That and other things," she replied, leaving her answer vague as she picked up a sandwich.

"You're so good with kids. And teaching them to love books is a gift they'll have all their lives." He took a bite of sandwich and gazed at her thoughtfully. "I'm thinking of opening a music studio for kids. Sort of the same idea as your children's program, but giving kids the gift of music."

"Really? In Granite Ridge?"

He nodded. "Yes. I see a need for that there."

"Do you really want to stay in Granite Ridge? You could perform in more exciting places, in lots of interesting locations. Everyone loves your music."

He studied her. "There's that old saying 'there's no place like home.' It's true. Home is where your heart is. And like Charlie says in his book, it's where family is too."

Hailey's eyes filled unexpectedly. He'd remembered what she'd written with such deep feelings. "Yes, I know that all too well. I love my family—the family that chose to welcome me in it."

He reached across the table and took hold of her hand. "I've heard the story of you Kirby sisters. It's beautiful. My mother knew Maddie as a little girl and always thought she was someone special."

Hailey blinked back her tears. She was being emotional, but it touched her heart to hear him say such nice things about the woman she adored.

"Hey, now," he said, rising and pulling her into his arms. "No tears. It's all happy."

She laid her head against his broad chest and sighed. Exactly as before, she felt at home in his arms. She didn't know if this was the true love Alissa talked about, but it felt good.

"Okay, let's work on the music," said Nick, giving her a last pat on the back. "I've worked up a simple tune and what I think will be the first verse. If you like it, maybe you can help me with another verse."

"That sounds like fun," said Hailey, wiping the last trace of tears from her face. She appreciated being able to be so open with him.

In the living room, Hailey took a seat on the couch while Nick slid onto the stool behind the keyboard.

He played a cheerful tune. And then he put words to it:

"Charlie and his dog, Zeke, too
    Have lots of ideas for you
    If you want to sing a song,
    Go ahead, just do it, do it, do it …
    Do, re, mi, la, ti, do,
    You don't need to be a super star

Because you're wonderful as you are"

Hearing some of her own words in the song, Hailey gaped at him, touched to the core.

"Well? What do you think?"

"I'm in love …" she choked, "… I'm in love with it. It's perfect—perky and fun and meaningful. I love the music as well as the words."

A smile lit his face, bringing a sparkle to his eyes. "Simple words, simple tune, but I think it works. Here's the beginning of another verse but it needs some work:

"Charlie and his dog Zeke too
    Have lots of ideas for you
    If you want to do a magic trick
    Go ahead, just do it, do it, do it…
    Flip a card and count to ten
    You don't need to carry it far
    Because you're magical as you are"

Delighted, Hailey clasped her hands together. "These are great. Putting words to a song isn't the same as writing it down to read. I think the words fit the music beautifully."

"I wonder if Lee Merriweather will feel the same way," Nick said.

Hailey smiled. "I'm sure she will."

He came out from behind the keyboard. "Okay, help me think of other things kids like to do. I'll try to make up more verses. I figured probably six at the most."

He walked over and sat down on the couch beside her. "I was thinking that kids want to read. Maybe I could use that in some way."

"Good idea," said Hailey, trying not to react to the casual way he'd thrown an arm around her. "They also want to be grown up, but we can't have them thinking they can do things like drive cars."

He grinned and she returned his smile.

"How about skipping?" she suggested. "It used to be said that if a child could skip, he or she was ready to read."

"Okay, something like if you want to skip, just do it, one foot, second foot, three."

"To go fast you don't need a car; fast little speed-sters that you are," Hailey quipped.

Laughing, Nick pulled her closer. "You're so refreshing, Hailey. I've been searching for someone like you."

Thrilled by his words, she gazed up at him.

His dark eyes drew her in as he leaned closer and closer.

When his lips met hers, she felt a tremor go through her. His soft kiss grew into something more demanding. She responded by sliding her arms around his neck and leaning into him. Behind her closed eyes, she had the sensation of seeing magical lights as if the fireworks she felt inside were exploding.

When they finally pulled apart, Nick stared at her. "Wow!" he said softly.

She snuggled against him and lifted her face for another kiss, realizing she'd never really been kissed before. Not like this. Her whole body felt liquid and then on fire, filling her with a need she'd never known to this extent. Confused and embarrassed by her reactions, she pulled away, needing to be on steadier ground.

"What's wrong?" Nick asked, giving her a worried look.

"Nothing. Absolutely nothing. That's why I think I'd better go."

He frowned. "Did I do something to make you uncomfortable?"

"I really want to stay, but it's best if I go. I think you probably know how I feel about you. But I don't do anything in a halfhearted way, and I see how it is with you and all those female fans. You can have your choice of any of them. Why would you choose me?"

He cupped her face in his strong hands. "Ah. You have no idea how lovely you are. It's something I really like about you." He stood and trailed a hand through his dark curls. "Look, we can move as slowly as you want, until you're ready."

Feeling awkward and fighting an unexplainable urge to cry, Hailey got to her feet. "Guess when the time is right, we'll both know it."

"Yeah, that's one way to put it." His disappointment was obvious.

Nick helped her into her coat, and showed her the door. "Take care, Hailey. Let me know if I can do anything to help with your family while they're here."

"Okay." As she hurried down the path away from the cabin, she felt tears form icy trails on her face. God! She was such a fool to be so scared of exploring what was blossoming between them.

She hurried into the hotel to the elevator, hoping no one would notice how upset she was. On the uppermost floor of the building, where the suites were located, she raced to her room and stopped abruptly. A note was posted to her door.

"Hailey, call me immediately. Mom"

Heart pounding with alarm, she struggled with the room card, opened the door, and ran over to her phone.

She clicked on her mother's number and waited impatiently for her to answer.

Her mother picked up the call and said breathlessly, "Hailey? You won't believe what has happened. You'd better come to my room. Jed is here."

"Jed here? At the hotel? Why?"

"It seems he's defying his family and marrying Alissa. The wedding is on!"

A tide of happiness washed through Hilary. "Oh my God! Alissa must be thrilled. Hang on! I'm on my way!"

She ran to the Presidential Suite where Mom and Nan were staying and burst through the doorway. "Alissa! I'm so-o-o excited for you!" Hailey wrapped her arms around her and held her tight. Their tears blended.

"It's not perfect," said Alissa, her voice wobbly. "His parents aren't here, and they still refuse to come. But Jed told me he won't live without me."

"Wow! I've been so mad at him, and now, I want to hug him."

Alissa let out a soft chuckle. "I know exactly what you mean."

Hailey turned to her mom. "Tomorrow, I'll pick up my bridesmaid dress in town and anything else you or anyone might need."

"Thanks." Her mother smiled. "Let's hope everything goes without a hitch from this point."

Hailey couldn't stop grinning at Alissa. "Guess this is the true love you described to me, huh?"

The smile that spread across Alissa's face was answer enough.

Hailey's thoughts flew to Nick. Time would tell if what they were feeling was the real thing or simply a moment of lust.

Later, when Hailey got the chance to speak to Jed alone, she said, "Thank you so much for making my sister happy. But if you ever hurt her like that again, you'll have to answer to me and, I suspect, each sister in the family, along with my mom."

Jed nodded solemnly. "I understand. Believe me, it's been a battle with my parents. Something I never expected from them. Now that my father is dying, they think I should do as they want. But what they don't understand is the love between Alissa and me is real. I can't imagine living without her."

"True love," Hailey said.

"Yeah, as corny as it may sound, it's real—the kind that will never fade."

Hailey gave him an impulsive hug. "I'm happy for both of you."

"Thanks," Jed said. "It means a lot coming from you. I know how close you and Alissa are."

"I'm going to town tomorrow. Is there anything I can do for you?"

"Just be there for Alissa."

"I always will," Hailey responded.

CHAPTER 7

After dinner, Hailey went up to her room to get her coat, trying to decide what to say to Nick. He was used to women who knew what they wanted and weren't afraid to go after it. She, on the other hand, was a real novice at trying to get a man's attention. Before, she hadn't cared enough to go after one. But now, she certainly did.

The sounds of country music met Hailey as she drew near to the bar. Surprised, she walked inside. According to the sign on the banner above the stage, a group called "Easy Town" was playing.

She looked around for Nick. Not seeing him, she approached one of the bartenders. "Is Nick here?"

The woman gave her a knowing smile. "No, he's off tonight. He'll be back tomorrow."

Crestfallen, Hailey left the bar. Maybe it was for the best, she thought, as old insecurities crept into her mind. In many ways, she was still the eight-year-old girl who'd lost so much faith in others caring for her that she barely talked. Even now, writing words and painting pictures were still the most comfortable ways for her to communicate with others.

Hailey went to her room, took off her coat, and walked over to her computer. Working always centered her. She needed that tonight.

She began a story about Charlie and his friends decorating a Christmas tree. Soon, she was lost in the process of finding the right words for a toddler to understand. As she typed them in, a melody began to play in her head. She attempted to write down the notes, thinking if nothing else happened between Nick and her, they could still conjure up some kids' songs to go with her books.

When her vision grew blurry, she realized it was after midnight and stopped. Tomorrow was an important day. First, she'd go to town to pick up her bridesmaid dress and other items for the wedding, and then she was going to join Casey for an afternoon at the spa.

Lying in bed, Hailey thought of the last few days and her interactions with Nick. For the first time in her life, she thought she was falling in love, the true kind, like Alissa and Jed shared. Jed had disappointed them all, but he'd pulled through for Alissa. And Alissa was happier than she'd ever been.

As she fell asleep, her thoughts remained on a dark-haired, brown-eyed man who sang and looked like a rock star, but who was gentle as could be with her.

The next morning after the family had breakfast together, Hailey made a list of things that she needed to get in town. She'd already decided to pick up some of her art supplies. Away from work and her busy schedule, ideas were forming in her mind for the Christmas book she was working on. Her agent would be thrilled.

Driving down the hill into town, she gazed at the beauty that surrounded her. The green boughs of pine trees and the stark branches of hardwood trees were iced with the light snow that had fallen during the night. Though she was a summer person at heart, winter days like this made her happy she lived in a place where all four of Mother Nature's seasons were celebrated.

From a distance above it, Granite Ridge looked like a miniature town set up by a Christmas tree. Charming is what most visitors called Granite Ridge. Home is what it was to Hailey and always would be.

Hailey drove to her condo. As usual, she experienced a moment of pride when she stepped inside. This lovely place was hers because she'd dared to dream she could tell stories and draw pictures that others would like.

She walked into her bedroom and went over to her closet. The long, blue-gray dress she was to wear as Alissa's maid of honor was as beautiful as always as she held it up in front of her. The dusty-blue, silky fabric and simple lines of the sleeveless dress she'd covered with a protective plastic bag were stunning and well suited to her smaller figure. She'd been given a gray shawl to wear over it to fend off the chill. She picked up the shawl and the sparkly silver shoes she'd chosen to wear and brought all of it to the living room to package up and take with her.

Then she went into her office and placed a sketch pad, along with colored pencils and charcoal into one of the canvas bags she had for such things and carried it out to the living room.

She stood there a moment, undecided, and then went back to her bedroom, opened her lingerie drawer and pulled out the black lacy bra and panties she'd tucked away, just in case Nick was the right person to see her in them.

Smiling at the thought, she trotted to the living room and carefully placed them with her art supplies.

Before she left town, Hailey headed to Hensley's Sweet Shoppe. Everyone had loved the Christmas Kisses she'd handed out. Time for a few more.

As usual, Stacy was behind the counter when she walked inside. Stacy smiled at her. "Hey, Hailey! I hear Lee Merriweather might have some competition for my brother's affection. Wouldn't that be something?"

Hailey felt heat stream to her cheeks. "Is that what he told you?"

"Sort of. In bits and pieces. You know how guys

are. They never tell you much. But it's definitely the impression I got. Let's hope it's true."

Hailey simply nodded, though excitement filled her.

"What can I get you? More Christmas Kisses?"

Hailey grinned. "Yes, everyone loves them. I'll take another box."

After she'd been served and paid, Hailey all but skipped out of the store. Nick had mentioned her. Maybe those black panties and bra were going to come in handy, after all. If she got another chance to be with Nick, she was going to take it.

Back at the lodge, the whole atmosphere seemed to have changed with the excitement of Alissa's upcoming wedding. The Christmas music sounded sweeter, the colors brighter, the lights more sparkly.

In her room, Hailey carefully hung up her dress and put away her things. Then she called Casey.

"Hey, girl! Are we set for the spa this afternoon?" Casey said.

"Yes. I can't wait!" said Hailey. "Why don't I meet you there now? We can eat a light lunch at the spa during our treatments. Bring a bathing suit for the pool. It's delightful to be able to lounge there."

"Will do. I can't wait to hear all about the change of plans for Alissa. It sounds so romantic."

Hailey's lips curved as they did every time that

she thought about it. "Romance is definitely in the air. I have a lot to tell you."

After a full body massage, Hailey sat in her bathing suit and a terry robe at a small table in a room they called The Greenhouse eating a salad and sipping cucumber water. Every muscle in her body was whispering *'thank you'* to her for the way they'd been pampered. Following lunch, she and Casey planned to sit in the garden pool and relax before having their facials. Spending money or time like this was something new for Hailey. She'd always been frugal, but after succeeding with her books, she'd begun budgeting for things like this. Tomorrow, she'd have her nails done with Alissa. Today was pure hedonistic pleasure.

Casey smiled at her. "Let's finish here, get in the pool, and then I'm going to pump you for plotting ideas for my next book."

"Okay. That should be fun. I loved your last book. Is it another book in the series?"

"Yes. But it's not going well. I'm stuck on a plot idea that I don't think will work."

"I have Alissa do a read-through for me. As a kindergarten teacher, she's good at picking up details I sometimes miss."

"Lucky you. And your sister, Jo, is your lawyer. Right?"

Hailey grinned. "Yes. Believe me, nothing gets past her."

"Double lucky. It's so nice you have sisters who will help you. I'm an only child."

Hailey grew pensive. "Yes, I'm very fortunate." She could've told Casey about her early years but decided not to. They were having too much fun to spoil it with those ugly facts.

They got up from the table and carried their water with them to the soaking pool.

Settling into the hot water, Hailey let out a sigh of appreciation. She liked being in the mountains but loved to find ways to keep warm from the cold air that tended to seep into her body. She faced Casey, who'd become such a good friend. "Okay, let's talk plot. Tell me what you have in mind."

A good twenty minutes later, Casey beamed at Hailey. "Okay, thanks. I think I've got it. This should work. Writing fantasy is such fun, but you have to be very careful to stick to the world you've built."

Hailey drew a deep breath. "You and Eric seem so happy. How do you know if what you have between you is the real thing?"

Casey chuckled. "Sometimes I think I'm crazy to think he's the one, and then I know I'm crazy in love with him. The good thing is he makes me a better person. I'm kinder, gentler, and more excited about life with him. Does that make sense?"

Hailey nodded. "It does."

Casey narrowed her eyes. "Is this about Nick?"

Feeling suddenly self-conscious, Hailey nodded.

"I think about him all the time. But with all the other girls interested in him both before he came back home and now, I wonder if he'll be able to accept me as I am."

"Why wouldn't he?" asked Casey scowling at her.

"I lead a pretty quiet life. And I like living in Granite Ridge."

"Ah. Well, that's something the two of you have to work out. The other stuff is already clear to me. He's definitely into you."

"I hope so," said Hailey, her voice suddenly shaky. "Because I think he might be the man I've waited for all this time."

Casey studied her. "You've got it bad, girl. But it'll turn out the way it's meant to be. I'm pretty sure I know exactly how."

Hailey returned her smile and hoped she was right because as Casey said, she had it bad for Nick.

At Jed's request, Hailey, her sisters, and her mom, joined him and Alissa for dinner that evening in a private section of the main dining room.

Hailey knew Jed was hurting, and she was glad to support him and his decision to break away from his family to marry Alissa. It was important for him to understand that once you became part of the Kirby family, it was forever, through trials and triumphs.

She gazed at her sister sitting next to him. Happiness bathed Alissa's face, giving her a glow that had been sorely missed. Hailey was relieved to know that things were going to be all right. If Alissa was forced to fight with Jed's family in the future, she'd stay strong. Having almost lost Jed once, Alissa wouldn't let it happen again.

After everyone had ordered their meal and were sipping wine or other drinks, Jed rose to his feet and tapped on his water glass for silence.

Putting a hand on Alissa's shoulder, he spoke. "I want to apologize to all of you for what has happened. As you now know, my father is dying. I was told I had to step into the family business and take over for him immediately. I'm aware of the need to do so, but I informed my parents I couldn't do it without the woman I love at my side. In time, they'll understand. Anyone who has met Alissa realizes what a treasure she is." His eyes filled. "She's my everything, you know?"

Hailey nodded with the others, her own eyes tearing up at the tender look he gave Alissa before leaning over and kissing her.

He sat down and studied each of them. "I'll make it up to Alissa and you. I swear I will."

"We are all here to support the two of you," said Mom. "I know you both love each other very much, and that you're both committed to making this work. And, Jed, I'll hold you to it."

"Yes, ma'am," he replied, giving her a little salute.

Everyone laughed at the gesture. Mom was a gentle soul but brooked no nonsense from anyone, not even someone who was about to become her son-in-law.

Hailey took a bite of her scrumptious filet mignon, her mind whirling. The way Jed kept looking at Alissa with such tenderness was certainly a sign of true love. She wanted Nick to look that way at her.

CHAPTER 8

The next evening, Hailey checked herself in the mirror—jeans, cowboy boots, flannel shirt to go with the country theme of the meal. She checked her watch and grabbed her coat, anxious to get there ahead of everyone else in the family. The rehearsal dinner was being held at Jackson's Pub with Stevie helping to prepare the barbeque and other food Jed had requested. A low-key country boy at heart, Jed had been delighted with the arrangements.

Outside, the air was frigid. There'd been talk of a snowstorm coming soon, but the system had stalled off the Pacific coastline, and not even the weather predictors knew if and when it would arrive.

Hailey hurried to the restaurant.

Inside, warm air and delicious aromas met her. She saw Nick working on something to do with music for the place and moved toward him, her heart racing.

When Nick saw her, he smiled. "What are you doing here?"

"I'm here for Alissa's rehearsal dinner." She drew in a shaky breath and let it out. "I want to apologize for running out on you like that. It's complicated. I have trust issues."

His brown-eyed gaze drilled into her. "I understand. Trust is a big thing for me too."

Hailey swallowed hard and then forced the words. "I want to spend more time with you." She waited for him to respond. For her, saying something like this was a big deal, exposing herself to rejection. She hoped he'd understand.

He nodded slowly. "Okay. Let's give it a try. I know you'll be busy tomorrow with the wedding and then there's Christmas …"

"I'm having Christmas brunch with my family, but if you're here on the mountain, we could meet in the afternoon." Her words were coated with hope.

"I'm not sure I'll be here then. It depends on what Stacy has planned for Regan. I'll let you know."

"All right. We'll wait and see," said Hailey, hiding her disappointment. She gave him a little wave and headed to the corner of the restaurant where the family was being seated.

"Wow! You and Nick are really getting along," said Stevie, coming up to her. "Want to tell us about it?"

"Absolutely not," said Hailey, laughing at the knowing looks Stevie was giving her.

Throughout the dinner served family style, Hailey laughed and joked with the others

enjoying this special time, but her thoughts remained on Nick, thrilled he was willing to meet with her sometime in the next couple of days.

When Hailey could eat no more of the delicious food, she patted her stomach and sat back to listen to the music coming through the speakers. Growing up, she'd learned to love all kinds of music. Country was among her favorites. Especially when a guy looking like Blake Shelton was singing his heart out to the crowd.

"Not bad, huh?" said Jo, dabbing her mouth with a napkin. "The food was so good I ate too much, but I don't care."

Hailey grinned at her. Jo was usually so serious. She liked seeing her like this.

When Alissa and Jed rose to leave, Hailey did too. She wanted to get back to her room to work on the Christmas book. Being here at the lodge was prompting all sorts of ideas for her latest one.

It wasn't until she was lying in bed that night, reliving her conversation with Nick, that a thought hit her like a blow to the head. Nick has said trust was a big thing for him. What would he think when he found out she was Lee Merriweather?

Hailey awoke to brilliant blue skies. Lying in bed, she smiled at the thought that Alissa would have such a lovely day for her wedding. Just thinking of the ceremony, she felt excitement weave through her. The first of the sisters to get married, Alissa would show them how special marriage could be.

Her phone rang. *Alissa.*

She answered it. "Hi! What a beautiful morning for your wedding!"

"I can't believe it's finally happening. You're going to meet me at the spa to get our nails done, right?"

"Yes, at our scheduled appointment. In addition to nails, I've hired someone to come to your room before the wedding to do our makeup. I really need help because I usually wear so little."

"Great. Okay … I'll meet you at the spa later."

"Alissa? I love you. I know you're going to be the perfect bride."

Alissa laughed. "I don't know about perfect, but thanks."

They clicked off the call, and Hailey scrambled out of bed. She'd left out her drawings for the book, hoping by letting them rest for a day, that more ideas for details would come later.

When she went down to the dining room, the place was alive with activity. A Christmas Eve Buffet was planned for hotel guests and at the far end of the room, tables were being set up for it.

Hailey followed the waitress to a small table and sat, content to watch the staff work and to admire the bright panorama out the window. The sun on the snow made the little ice crystals atop it sparkle as if fairy dust had been spread everywhere. In the valley below, Granite Ridge was bustling with holiday activity. Hailey thought of Regan and the other little children in the story time group and wondered if they were as excited as she used to be. Her first Christmas with her sisters would always remain a memory to be treasured.

Later, with her nails done a dusty blue to match her dress, Hailey went to Alissa's room to get her makeup done before the ceremony. Alissa and Jed had chosen to get married in a private corner of the lobby, beautifully sheltered by the large Christmas tree.

As she, Alissa, and Mom were getting dressed, Jo and Stevie arrived with a bottle of champagne and several glasses.

"Time to celebrate," said Jo, as she waited for Stevie to open the bottle of bubbly wine.

Hailey stood with the others while the wine was poured into glasses and handed out.

Stevie lifted her glass. "Here's to Alissa on her wedding day."

"And to all of us who love her," added Hailey.

Jo clicked her glass against Hailey's. "To the soul sisters!"

After Alissa thanked them, Mom said, "I'm

proud of you all, my beautiful, lovely girls. I see you all wearing the pearl necklaces I gave you for your high school graduations. It makes me wonder where the time has gone." Her eyes filled. "Now let's end this emotional journey before I ruin my makeup."

Amid the laughter that followed, Hailey savored this moment. They were lucky to be together. Even after Alissa was married, Hailey knew they'd all remain close.

During the ceremony, Hailey stood next to Alissa as she faced Jed, ready to repeat her vows. Mitch Morris, one of Jed's best friends who'd just flown in for the ceremony, stood on the other side of Jed.

She'd heard different wedding vows exchanged before, but now Hailey listened to every word carefully, trying to evaluate them for further use with Nick, if she were lucky enough to get to this point.

Out of the corner of her eye, she observed each of her sisters, Mom, and Nan. They all wore tender expressions as they listened as carefully as she. After words of love and commitment were given, hugs were exchanged all around.

Alissa's eyes shimmered with emotion. "Thank you, everyone." She turned to Jed with a smile and accepted another kiss from him.

The photographer they'd hired to take pictures asked them all to line up by the Christmas tree. After taking several shots of various groupings inside and out by the lit gazebo, the photographer was done.

"Okay, time to celebrate," said Mom.

Hailey and the others headed up the winding stairway to the gourmet restaurant. A special room had been set aside for them.

A hostess greeted them at the entrance and led them to a small, private dining room that had been dressed with greens, blue-gray ribbons, and an assortment of white flowers, including white orchids, camellias, and snow drops. On the long, white-linen-covered table, a Calla Lily sat in a crystal vase at each place, matching the simple centerpiece of lilies, greens, and pine cones that had been dipped in silver.

Hailey gasped at the beauty of the room.

She found her place next to Alissa and took a seat. Mitch was seated on the other side of Jed. She smiled at him. Though she hadn't seen much of him, he seemed like a really nice guy.

Across the table from her sat Mom and Nan. Her sisters filled in, making Hailey feel very grateful to be part of the celebration.

The wine steward came into the room carrying a silver bucket on a stand. He pulled a green bottle from the bucket and showed it to Mom.

At her nod of approval, he proceeded to uncork the bottle with a pleasing soft sound. He then poured a small amount of the white, bubbly wine into her glass and waited for her to react.

She took a sip and smiled. "Excellent. Thank

you." She turned to the others. "There's nothing like a delicious champagne to celebrate this special day."

Mom waited for another bottle to be opened and for everyone to be served the champagne and then she raised her glass. "Here's to Alissa and Jed. May they have many happy years ahead of them. We love you both so much."

Murmurs and congratulations filled the air.

Then Mitch got to his feet. "I've known Jed for a long time and I've never seen him happier than he is today. And no wonder, he's now a part of this wonderful family who's accepted him as he is." He gave Jed a devilish grin. "Warts and all. Too many things to talk about here."

Hailey joined in the laughter. Then it was her turn.

She stood and stared a moment at Alissa, reveling in her happiness. Her gaze traveled around the room to the faces of those so dear to her. "A wedding is a time when love is declared for one another. Alissa and Jed have exchanged vows of their love and devotion made more meaningful because it almost didn't happen. But I've seen now that what they share is true and meaningful, that the future is brighter and better for them having gone through this trial." She fought tears as she continued. "There is no better way to celebrate this time of happiness for them than with family. Mom and Nan opened their hearts to me and my sisters from the beginning. When I wonder how best to describe love, I think of them and each of you, my wonderful, precious soul sisters."

Too emotional to continue, she sat back down and noticed that everyone in the room was wiping their eyes.

The dinner went as smoothly as the wedding. After being part of a friend's large wedding, Hailey realized how much easier a small, simple wedding was. In this case, there were no disagreements, no bridezilla actions. Alissa's face was flushed with happiness that seemed to grow every time she looked at her new groom.

When it came time for dessert, Hailey and everyone grew quiet, anxious to see what Stevie had made for the wedding cake. As a child, Stevie had loved to bake and be active in the kitchen, then she'd worked in various places in professional kitchens. Though Stevie never thought of herself as a true chef, Hailey and everyone else in the family believed she fit the description perfectly whenever they tasted her food.

Hailey sighed with pleasure at the sight of the elegant, two-tiered cake iced in the most subtle of blue, like a whisper of the dusty color Alissa favored. In addition to the decoration that looked like wide lace ribbon circling each tier, Stevie had placed white camellias, silver leaves, and tiny pinecones with dusty blue berries on the front of the cake. A bride and groom stood atop the cake beside the spill of tiny silver pinecones.

Hailey leaned closer. The bride and groom looked exactly like Alissa and Jed.

"Beautiful!" Hailey exclaimed. "Stevie, you are so

clever! Is it our favorite? White cake with layers of raspberry and cream filling?"

Color flooded Stevie's cheeks at the compliments flying toward her. She nodded happily.

Later, after Alissa and Jed had cut the cake and they'd all eaten their fill of the scrumptious master-piece, Hailey said, "What about the bouquet? Alissa, you have to toss it!"

"I haven't forgotten it," said Alissa. She handed it to Stevie. "Here, I want you to have it."

"Me?" Stevie's eyebrows popped in horror. "You should give it to someone who might actually use it someday."

"No," said Alissa. "You're the one who's made this wedding so special with all your hard work. I want you to have it."

Stevie's cheeks flushed. "Okay . . . well, thank you. I'll keep it safe until one of you needs it."

"Whatever you say," said Alissa, giving her pink cheek a kiss. "It's yours."

CHAPTER 9

Hailey walked up to her room feeling blue. She normally was content with her life, but since spending time with Nick, she realized she wanted someone special to share it with.

She entered the room and stared at herself in the full-length mirror, admiring the dress she and Alissa had chosen for her to wear as maid of honor. The dusty grey-blue color offset her strawberry-blond hair and brought out the color of her eyes. The makeup artist had done a nice job of not overdoing it. She fingered her pearl necklace, another nice touch to her outfit.

A knock at the door caught her attention.

She left the bedroom and hurried to answer it. She cracked the door open and stepped back in surprise.

"Hi, Nick! What are you doing here?"

He grinned at her. "Wow!"

Flustered, she chuckled. "Nice to see you. Come on in."

"Thanks. I came to invite you to my cabin tomorrow at four o'clock for a Christmas supper. Stacy and Regan will be with friends, so I'm free."

"Thank you. I'd love to come. Would you like something to drink? There are drinks and sodas in the room refrigerator."

He shook his head. "I can't. I'm on duty. There's a problem with lighting in one of the guest rooms." He glanced over at the table where she'd been working. "What are you doing?"

Hailey froze. "It's just something I was working on," she said, trying to act casual though her pulse was racing so fast she thought she might faint.

"Can I see?" Without waiting for her permission, he walked over to where her drawings were laid out and turned to her wide-eyed. "Wait a minute! Those pictures are of Charlie and some of his friends. How? … Oh …"

Color left his face and came back in a rush. He narrowed his eyes at her. "*You* are Lee Merriweather?"

Observing his angry scowl, Hailey clasped her hands together like a prayer. "I was going to tell you, but the chance never came up."

"Not true, Hailey. You had plenty of opportunities to tell me." He shook his head. "You've gone and made a fool of me."

"No! I wanted you to get to know *me*, not Lee

Merriweather," she countered, feeling sick to her stomach.

"You couldn't trust me?" The hurt in his voice pierced her.

"It's not like that," Hailey said, scrambling to find the right words.

"How is it then?" he snapped.

She swallowed hard. "It's complicated. It doesn't really have anything to do with you."

"Oh yes, it does. I thought we were becoming friends. Maybe a lot more. You know how I feel about trust. We've already talked about it." He drew his fingers through his dark curls and emitted a sound that was rougher than a sigh. "Look, I've gotta go to work. Too bad this happened. I thought we had something special going on." He turned and headed for the door.

Hailey rushed to him and took hold of his arm. "Don't go! We can talk about this."

When his gaze met hers, there was little warmth in his eyes. "Like I said, I have to get back to work. Any talk will have to wait."

He walked out, closing the door firmly behind him, leaving her standing alone in the entry feeling crushed. Nick thought her silence was deception. But, for her, it was protection.

Hailey took off the dress that had made her feel so beautiful and climbed into bed, too emotionally exhausted to do any more. The image of Nick's face exhibiting his disappointment in her played over and over in her mind. She doubted she'd get any sleep, but she had to try. Tomorrow was Christmas, and the family was getting together for their annual gathering, which would, no doubt, include a gift of pajamas or nightgowns from Mom.

The next morning, Hailey joined her sisters and Nan in her mother's suite. Mom had placed a number of gifts under the tree, including a bag of them Hailey had given her to hand out. Each year, Hailey spent a long time choosing a present for each of her sisters, Nan, and Mom. Though she kept it to the family rule of a maximum of fifty dollars, Hailey was a bargain hunter who found her gifts throughout the previous year.

This year, she'd chosen a special, different book for each family member, along with a soft cashmere wrap she'd found on sale online. Pleased with the idea of giving them hours of pleasure with cozy reading, she could hardly wait to see their reactions.

Her thoughts flew back to the first Christmas they'd shared and how she'd carefully chosen gifts for her sisters. She remembered how excited they'd all been and decided not to let her quarrel with Nick ruin the spirit of the day.

As they gathered around the special little Christmas tree in the room, Mom handed each of them a package. "Go ahead, girls. Open them up."

"Wonder what this is," teased Stevie.

"Let's see, we've recently had snowmen, angels,

and reindeer in a variety of colors," said Jo. She glanced at her mother with a roguish smile. "I'm waiting for leopard pajamas."

Everyone laughed.

"I'm guessing stripes," Hailey said, ripping open her package. "Yes!" She held up the green striped pajamas trimmed in red.

Laughing, she and the other girls changed into their pajamas for their annual photos.

"It doesn't seem the same without Alissa," Jo said with a note of sadness.

"Guess it's always going to be different from now on," Hailey said. "It's Alissa this year. Who's going to be next?"

It wasn't until later that Hailey realized no one ever answered or looked her in the eye.

"I've ordered brunch to be delivered to my suite," said Mom. "I thought we'd have more privacy here. The food should be coming soon."

"Good idea," said Jo. "I have plans later, but this time with the family is important to me."

"Me, too," said Hailey, keeping her plans with Nick private. Who knew if he would even want to see her?

While they were exchanging gifts, the room service wait staff came into the suite and set up their meal buffet style on the dining room table in Mom's huge Presidential Suite.

After they left, Mom announced it was time to help themselves.

Hailey eagerly selected a number of food items,

including scrambled eggs, bacon, and a warm biscuit with blueberry jam made from locally grown blueberries.

Later, sipping coffee, she relaxed on the couch and listened to the chatter of her sisters. She'd been quiet as a child and was still content to sit by as others talked.

Full of food and good cheer, Hailey left her mother's suite with her arms full of gifts. Because she hadn't slept well the night before, she was looking forward to a nap.

After getting things settled in her room, still in her pajamas, she crawled into bed.

Minutes later, she was up again. The memory of Nick's anger kept her too restless to sleep. Giving in to reality, she took a hot shower and dressed for the day in jeans and the new warm sweater that Mom had given her, declaring it matched her eyes.

She gazed at the sketches she'd roughly drawn and put them in sequence. Her picture books were the normal thirty-two pages. Wondering how the story was going to end, she picked up her charcoal and began to sketch ideas. Charlie and his friends were looking for the perfect thing to put on the top of the tree, different from a star or an angel, an object that signified something wonderful about Christmas magic.

As the time neared four o'clock, Hailey tensed. Would Nick call or text her and tell her not to come?

By four fifteen, Hailey felt comfortable enough to put on her coat and head out the door. As embarrassed and worried as she was, she knew she had to give Nick an explanation for keeping her identity a secret if she wanted their relationship to continue.

As she walked past the lobby, she saw groups of people chatting or sitting in one of the comfortable chairs or sofas, filling the room with the happy sounds of contented guests. No wonder, the lobby inside was striking with its holiday decorations, and the music through hidden speakers was cheerful.

Outside, a few lazy snowflakes floated to the ground. So far, the storm that had been predicted hadn't shown any signs of arriving. Her breath caught. She was used to winter weather in the valley, but mountain air was different—clearer, colder.

The lights on the Christmas tree in the front circle winked at her, as if they knew how uncertain she was about appearing on Nick's doorstep.

She crunched through the snow, following the path into the woods to where his and a few other cabins for the staff lay scattered beneath the tall firs.

At the door to his cabin, cold that had nothing to do with the outdoors raced through her body. She drew a deep breath.

Telling herself to be brave, she lifted her hand and knocked.

He flung open the door and waved her in. "It's cold out there. Better come inside."

Not the welcome she was hoping for. She stepped over the threshold and stood facing him as he shut the door behind her. "I … I wasn't sure you'd still want me to come here."

He sighed and shook his head. "We need to talk."

She unzipped her jacket and allowed him to help her out of it. *Might as well get this over with*, she thought, certain he was about to break off their tenuous relationship.

He put an arm around her. "C'mon. It's not that bad. Let me take your coat. I've opened a bottle of wine and have the fire going. Come sit on the couch with me."

She followed him and sat down, grateful for the warmth seeping into the room from the fireplace.

"Merry Christmas," Nick said, handing her a glass of wine and lifting his own glass.

"Yes, Merry Christmas," Hailey answered stiffly, wondering why he was being so nice if he was going to break things off with her.

After taking a sip of wine, Nick set his glass down. "I need to know why you wouldn't trust me with the knowledge that you were Lee Merriweather. Especially when you knew how I felt about her … your … work."

Trying to find the words, Hailey took another sip of wine. Though she seldom talked about her past, she knew she owed it to him to do it now.

"It's going to take a while," she cautioned him.

"No problem. Dinner is being kept warm in the oven. Take all the time you need."

Hailey stared into the fire and started talking. "Maddie Kirby took me in when I was eight-years-old, a scared kid who never knew when someone might hit me. I'd been in two previous foster homes —one not so good, the other worse. I learned to think thoughts in my head so I wouldn't speak them aloud and bring attention to myself. I had no reason to trust anyone. Over time, Mom was able to give that gift to me. But I'll always be cautious."

She drew in air and let out a shaky breath. "I was a skinny kid with funny hair and thick glasses. The kids who dared to make fun of me soon found out my sisters were watching out for me, and it stopped. Teachers discovered my imagination and my gift of drawing and put me to work, helping me to get my painful story out. Once I felt freer from the past, I made friends, but I've always felt people needed to earn my trust. Putting a name on a book of mine was one of the biggest leaps of faith I've ever made. Of course, I wasn't so brave as to put my own name on it. But still, it was a big deal for me."

"In time, people will find out who Lee Merri-weather really is," said Nick. "It's inevitable because your books are so good."

"I know now that people aren't making fun of the books, that they really like them. So, my next book will let readers know a bit about the real me."

"Good." Nick studied her. "I'm sorry you've had such a hard time of it. I wish there were a way I could take all that hurt away from you."

She nodded, touched by his kindness.

He took hold of one of her hands. "Hailey, I need to know if you're willing to trust me. Now, not later, not maybe, but trust me in every way."

The tears that had filled her eyes trailed down her face as she gave him a steady look. "Yes, I understand … but I needed to know your interest in me was real, not your being dazzled by the idea of Lee Merriweather."

"I see how you are with Regan and the other children, and I feel as if I know you. Your very soul is in the books I've read to Regan over and over again. So once again, I'm asking if you're willing to trust me."

Gazing into his eyes, Hailey knew with certainty that he would never harm her. "Yes, oh yes, I do trust you," she said reaching for him. He was the best, the kindest man she'd ever allowed herself to become close to.

He drew her to him and kissed the top of her head. "I know it sounds crazy, but in these past few days, spending time with you, you've … I don't know … captured me."

She leaned away and studied his face, forcing herself to ask the question that would always haunt her if it went unanswered. "Me or Lee Merriweather?"

His lips curved into a sexy grin. "The one I'm holding in my arms."

"But …"

"There's no reason to doubt my feelings for you, Hailey. After all the crap I've been through with female fans, I realize you're the kind of woman I've always wanted. That's why it seems so right for me to feel the way I do."

"We're just beginning to know one another," said Hailey.

"That's something I want to correct as soon as possible." He gave her a penetrating look, reaching inside her to the part of her she usually kept safe from others.

"Me too," she murmured as his lips came down on hers.

Every nerve ending in her body came alive as he continued to kiss her in a way that told a story of his own loneliness and how he truly felt about her.

He pulled away and cupped her face in his broad hands. "I've waited all my life for someone like you," he whispered in her ear, sending waves of joy through her.

"Someone?" she said, giving him a teasing smile.

His expression softened. "No, not someone. Just you." He wrapped an arm around her and drew her closer to him. "Now, tell me more about Hailey Kirby."

They talked and talked, sharing life experiences, hopes for the future, and the many ways that strengthened their bond.

After exhausting conversation, they lay together.

He trailed a finger over the features of her face. "You're beautiful, you know."

She smiled. He made her feel so good.

When she reached out to him, he settled in her

arms and began to show her what she'd been missing all her life.

Later, Hailey cuddled up against him. Nick had talked about knowing her soul. Now, she felt the same way about him.

When he noticed her tears, he pulled away. "Did I hurt you?"

She shook her head. "No, it's just that you've made me so happy."

"Is that why you're crying?" he teased as he gently brushed away a stray tear.

She gazed at him, loving him so much words were hard to find. "My heart is overflowing with lovely feelings—like Charlie when he found Zeke as a puppy. He knew they'd be good together for always." She kissed him and whispered, "Like us."

"I've fallen so hard for you," he murmured as their lips met.

Sometime later, Nick's stomach rumbled loudly. "Guess we'd better get our dinner."

Hailey chuckled, suddenly hungry herself. It had been hours since she'd arrived at the cabin. She rose and stared at her clothes scattered on the floor.

"Here, take one of my clean shirts," said Nick, handing her a short-sleeved black T-shirt.

Hailey slid it over her head and laughed at her image in the mirror. On her, it looked like a mini dress. She wrapped her arms around herself and inhaled the spicy scent of Nick's aftershave that still clung to the shirt. This smell would always remind her of opening her heart to Nick and to what she already thought of as true love.

She padded into the kitchen and sat at the table watching Nick plate up what looked like a turkey dinner. One of her favorites.

"Can I help?" she asked.

"No, thanks. I've got this." He placed mashed potatoes and a vegetable mélange on a plate alongside sliced turkey and stuffing. "We can serve the gravy ourselves. Hope you like it."

"I will," said Hailey, accepting a plate of food from him.

He grinned and winked at her. "We can have the appetizers for dessert."

"That works just fine," she said, returning his smile, hardly able to believe she was there with him.

As if he read her thoughts, he wiggled his eyebrows. "With appetizers, we can start all over again."

She felt a flush creep up her cheeks at the memory of their lovemaking and laughed—a sound of pure delight.

CHAPTER 10

I t was dark and quiet when Nick walked Hailey
back to the lodge. He'd wanted her to stay the
night, but she needed to have some time to
herself. He had the next few days off work, and she'd
agreed to stay with him then.

After they shared a sweet kiss, she made her way
out of the lobby elevator onto her floor, she moved
quietly along the hallway to her room, hoping not to
disturb anyone at this late hour.

Inside her room, Hailey tossed her coat on a chair,
flung off her boots and did a little dance across the
sitting area. She was in love. She couldn't and
wouldn't deny it, and wished she had someone to
tell. Casey and Eric were gone. Alissa was well occu-
pied with Jed. And she wasn't quite ready to talk to
Mom or her sisters about it. They'd all been pretty
quiet and off by themselves this vacation, as if they
really needed a break. Hailey respected that.

Hailey went into the bedroom and took off her

clothes. Studying herself in the mirror, she looked at her body with a new appreciation. It was almost magical the way tenderly giving and receiving love melded souls. Trust was a part of it, but so much more was involved.

After dinner, Nick had talked to her a little bit about his pleasant childhood in Granite Ridge, the sadness when his father died and then his mother, his sister's unreliable ex-husband, and why he felt a commitment to both Stacy and Regan to try and make them happy. He was such a good man. Her man.

Hailey drew hot water in the bathtub for a soak. Sitting in water sometimes helped her plot books and come up with new ideas. Tonight, she just wanted to relax and think of the miracle she'd discovered in Nick. No wonder he loathed the traveling life of a rock band guitarist and singer. He'd grown up in Granite Ridge and was a hometown family guy.

She lay back in the water and rested her head on the rounded edge of the tub, trying to get comfortable. She replayed the conversations with Nick. He'd been very open with her about the fact his father had traveled a lot and was gone most of the time before he died at a fairly young age. His mother, Beverly, was the person who'd made the Sweet Shoppe successful. And now Stacy was carrying on the family business. With Regan's father out of the picture, Nick wanted to be a presence in Regan's life. She admired him for that.

Her thoughts moved on to their lovemaking. He

matched every hero she'd ever read about in romance books. Now, in the stillness of the room, Hailey sighed and wiggled her toes with pleasure.

When at last she got out of the tub, she dried herself and crept into bed feeling as if she could sleep for a week.

But the next morning, when the sun poked through the curtains she'd forgotten to close tightly, thoughts of spending the next few days with Nick had Hailey eagerly getting up. Last night had been incredible.

Downstairs, she grabbed a quick breakfast at the coffee café. In the lobby, people in skiing gear milled around, anxious to get up to the top of the mountain and begin a day on the slopes.

Hailey texted Mom to ask her if they could meet for coffee. Hailey knew how she felt about Nick, but she really wanted to get her mother's perspective on her relationship with him. She'd needed Alissa's input on love, but she needed assurance from her mother that she wasn't being foolish.

When her mother walked into the coffee shop, warmth filled Hailey's heart. Maddie was the best mom any girl could have—loving, kind, honest.

"Thanks for coming, Mom," said Hailey. "May I get you a cup of coffee or tea?"

"Thanks. Coffee sounds delightful." Her mother studied her. "Everything all right, Hailey?"

Hailey couldn't stop a smile from spreading across her face. "I think so. Stay right there. I'll be right back with our drinks."

She hurried over to the service counter, ordered two cups of coffee, and carried them back to her mother, her heart pounding in nervous beats. Her mother's opinion meant everything to her.

Hailey handed her mother her coffee, placed her own cup of coffee on the table in front of them, and studied her mother's beautiful face.

"I've been spending time with Nick Hensley," she began. "You remember my crush from when I was a kid?"

"Yes, of course, I remember Nick. He and his sister have taken over the candy shop for their mother. But isn't he also in a rock band?"

"He was in a famous one, but is now living in Granite Ridge and working here at the lodge handling all their music and doing maintenance work. He's part of a local band, but it's only a part-time thing. He's through with traveling and performing on the bigger, national scene. He wants to settle down here in Idaho."

"And?" Mom cocked an eyebrow. "What are you really telling me, Hailey?"

Hailey clasped her hands together and closed her eyes. When she opened them, her eyes filled as she gazed at her mother. "I love him. And he loves me too."

"Isn't this quite sudden?" Mom asked.

"Yes and no. It seems that way but, in truth, I feel

like we've known each other forever. He loves my writing, and I love his music. We're even working on some songs together. It's as if I've finally found the special man I've been waiting for all my life. He's kind, hardworking, generous, and an all-around nice guy. I love him so much. Isn't that what it was like for you with your husband?"

Mom sat back against the chair and was quiet a moment as she stared into space. When she looked again at Hailey, she whispered, "Yes. It was exactly like that." She took hold of Hailey's hand. "But, Hailey, don't rush into anything. You've got plenty of time to let that relationship grow."

"I know. But I wanted to speak to you about it because I've never felt this way before, and it's happened so fast."

Mom hugged her. "Thanks for telling me. I love you." She brushed a curl away from Hailey's face. "And if this becomes all you want it to be, I'll be the first one cheering you on."

Hailey stood and wrapped her arms around her mother, relieved that things had gone so well because like it or not, she didn't need any more time to know how deep her feelings were for Nick.

After leaving her mother, Hailey went to her room and packed a few things to take to Nick's. She'd already decided to take her sketches and manuscript too. Now that he knew who Lee Merriweather was, she wanted to take advantage of any input Nick might be willing to give her. In return, she wanted to tell him about the melody that appeared in her head as she sketched this new story.

When she returned to the lobby, much of the early morning crowd was still gathered there. She looked, but didn't see any sign of her sisters and was happy to keep it that way. As sure as she felt about Nick, she didn't want them to know just yet. It was all so new, so unexpected.

She hurried along the path, checking the gray sky. She hadn't seen a weather report, but there was a smell of snow in the air. She told herself it might be nothing more than having all her senses come alive after being with Nick.

Nick met her at the door with a smile. He took the bags from her. "Come on in. I've got fresh coffee made. And early this morning, I went to town and stocked up on supplies, so we're all set to enjoy ourselves."

"Wow! You've got everything planned."

He laughed. "There's a storm coming. I wanted to be ready."

"Is it a big one?" she said, surprised.

"Yeah, it could be. But you know how it is with weather predictions in this area. The town may not get hit, but up here in the mountains, we probably will."

"Good thing I packed warm clothes." She gave him a tentative smile. "I hope to do a lot of fun things while I'm with you."

He winked at her. "I can think of a few."

She chuckled happily. "I mean outdoors, silly."

He laughed. "I brought my sister's ice skates here for you. Thought we could spend some time on the rink."

"Great. After the other day skating with my friend, Casey, I could use the practice."

They sat together in the kitchen sipping coffee, chatting comfortably about their usual routines.

"I've brought my art and writing supplies," said Hailey. "I thought you might help me with my Christmas story, and I have an idea for a song for you."

His eyes widened. "You'd trust me to help you?"

"Yes. Especially because you know Charlie better than anyone I know. You couldn't write songs for him if you didn't."

"So, we're to become a team of sorts?"

"Why not?" she said, realizing the giant step she was taking with Nick.

"Just checking," he said, his face alight with pleasure.

"Before we do any work, let's go outside. I don't want to get caught in any storm," said Hailey.

Nick got up. "Let me get those ice skates for you. Stacy also sent thick, warm woolen socks to wear with them."

"How sweet of her! I'm going to need them. My feet froze last time."

While Nick got the skates for her, Hailey rinsed out the coffee cups and put them in the dishwasher.

For a small cabin, it had every convenience anyone would want. Nick was lucky to have such living arrangements.

Nick returned with white figure skates for her and his black hockey skates. "Let's go! While I'm at the rink, I need to check on the sound system. Someone complained the music for skating was too soft."

"Before we leave, where should I put my things?"

"Put your suitcase in the bedroom and your work things in the corner behind the couch. If the kitchen table isn't large enough for you, I'll move things around later to give you space to work.

Hailey rolled her suitcase to the bedroom and stood a moment staring at the king-size bed. Things were moving fast, but as she'd promised herself earlier, she was going to enjoy these new life experiences. Best of all, she trusted Nick to abide by her wishes.

At the skating rink, she sat with others on a long bench inside The Skate Shack, which wasn't a shack at all. After she'd put on the thick socks and had laced her skates up, she stood and wiggled her toes. The skates fit perfectly.

Nick was busy talking to someone behind the desk, so she went outdoors and took a few practice circles. Soon, beautiful music played from the speakers placed strategically around the rink. She moved in rhythm to it, loving the feeling of the cold air on her cheeks as her body warmed up.

Suddenly someone was at her elbow. She turned to see Nick.

"May I have this dance?" he said, giving her a teasing grin.

"Why, of course," said Hailey, playing along.

They moved in perfect time together, matching their strides with the music. With Nick beside her, Hailey felt as if they really were dancing like some of the skating stars she admired.

She turned to him, caught the tip of her skate in the ice, and started to fall. Strong arms held her upright.

"Easy," Nick murmured. He put an arm around her waist, and steadier now, they moved forward.

"How about a break?" said Nick a bit later. "There's something I want to show you. It's one of my favorite places."

"Okay, I need a break," said Hailey. Her ankles were beginning to feel wobbly.

They went back to the shack and took off their skates.

"Let's have some hot soup," Nick said. "Then we can do a little hiking."

Hailey loaded their skates into a locker, reset the lock, and joined Nick at one of the tables.

He handed her a bowl. "This will warm you up. The tomato basil soup is my favorite."

She dug into it with enthusiasm. The hot mixture

coated her throat with warmth as it slid down, bringing her new energy.

Nick handed her a bottle of water. "We'll take this with us."

As she was eating, a little girl caught her eye. Hailey waved to her and, beaming, the girl waved back.

Nick chuckled. "You sure like kids. And they love you."

"Yes, they're so open and honest with you," Hailey said. "I'm sure some of the parents of kids at story time would be surprised to know what I've learned about them through their children. I have a number of funny stories."

"Speaking of stories," Nick said, taking hold of her hand. "I want you to know how much I like the idea of working together on both songs and the Christmas book. It means a lot to me that you believe in me."

"I know exactly what you mean. It took a lot of encouragement from others for me to begin to get serious about my books. I'm so glad I had that support. Publishing is a rough business, but when I hold one of my books in my hands, it's worth all the trouble and worry."

"I like it when a song finally makes sense," Nick said. "Regan loved the new song when I sang it to her."

"Did she have a wonderful Christmas?" Hailey asked.

"Yeah, she was excited about everything. I bought

her a bunch of toys and started a savings account for her."

"Good idea," said Hailey. She thought back to her first Christmas with Maddie, going to the store and holding a five-dollar bill in her hand. She'd never seen so much money.

They finished their soup and carried their water bottles out of the store.

"Okay, where are we going?" asked Hailey.

"Follow me. You'll see." Nick waved her forward and then turned to make sure she was coming. He led her through the thick trees near the rink.

Hailey was lagging behind when he swiveled around to face her.

Nick waited for her and then took her gloved hand. "Right ahead is a beautiful ledge that over-looks the valley. I come here to think. It's peaceful and quiet."

He led her to a rocky outcropping and brushed the snow off a large, flat-topped rock. "Have a seat."

She sat down and looked with wonder at the valley below. Though she could see movement, the only sound she could hear was the whispering of wind in the pine boughs of many of the trees around them.

Nick nudged her and raised a finger to his lips.

A rabbit hopped a distance away from them, unaware of their presence with the wind blowing toward them. As white as the snow, the rabbit could hardly be seen as it suddenly bounded away.

"Very peaceful," Hailey murmured, indicating the area with a sweep of her arm.

"Yes. A good place to think." He grinned at her. "I also get song ideas here too."

"Oh! Let me try to tell you about the melody that keeps running through my head." She gave him a sheepish grin. "Warning. I'm not a great singer."

She thought of her drawings for the Christmas book and began to hum.

Nick leaned closer. "Do that again."

She hummed the song.

Nick picked up on the tune and sang it aloud.

Hailey clapped her hands together. "That's it! Only better." She threw her arms around him. "You're so good!"

Laughing, he pulled her closer and lowered his lips to hers. In the cold air, his warm lips tasted wonderful.

When they finally pulled apart, they simply stared at one another, exchanging silly smiles.

"I can't get over our being together. It seems so right," Nick said, kissing the tip of her nose.

"Perfect," Hailey agreed.

He stood and helped her to her feet. "The sky is ripe with snow. We'd better head back."

She knew it was more than worry about a storm that was enticing them to leave for the cabin, and it was all right with her.

CHAPTER 11

A s they were walking to the cabin, snowflakes began to fly into their faces behind the strength of a strong wind that had picked up. Nick took hold of her hand in what was fast becoming a blinding storm. They stumbled through the woods into the cleared areas around the lodge and fought their way to the cabin. Though it was early in the afternoon, it seemed dark as night.

"I've never seen it snow like this," puffed Hailey, trying to keep up with Nick.

"It's a real blizzard," he replied. "I'm glad I brought supplies for us. We may be snowed in for a while."

Anticipation threaded through her. She couldn't think of anything more romantic than being trapped inside with Nick. By the time they reached the doorstep to his cabin, there were at least two inches of snow on the ground with no let-up in sight.

Nick unlocked the door, and they hurried inside.

They took off their wet hats and jackets and hung them on pegs on the wooden rack by the front entry and placed their boots on the special absorbent rug beneath the rack.

Hailey looked down at her pants. They were wet from the melting snow. "I'll be right back. I've got to change."

"Me, too," said Nick. He followed her into the bedroom.

Hailey took off her jeans and hung them in the bathroom. When she returned to the bedroom, Nick was standing by the bed wearing only a T-shirt and a pair of undershorts.

They stared at one another and then Nick moved toward her, his interest obvious.

He kissed. "I want you, Hailey."

She smiled. She'd waited all day to hear those words.

Sometime later, Hailey walked into the kitchen. Nick was at the stove, fixing some food.

He turned to her and grinned. "Hi, Sleepyhead!"

She smiled and stretched. "What time is it?"

"Almost six o'clock. I didn't dare disturb you. You looked so peaceful."

She raced to the front door and opened it. "Oh, my God! Look at all the snow!"

"Yes. Over a foot of it and more coming down."

"The weather people have been talking about a

storm for so long, I think we all forgot it might really happen," she said, closing the door firmly behind her.

"I've called the hotel and told them where I was in case they need me for an emergency. But with me technically on vacation, we can enjoy ourselves. I've got a fire going in the fireplace, and we have plenty of food and wine."

Hailey smiled at the idea of having all this privacy. She thought of checking in with her family and decided to simply send a text to Mom, telling her where she was.

She strolled into the kitchen, her thick socks acting like slippers against the wood floor.

"What are you making?"

"Spaghetti. I bought some sauce from Giuseppe's restaurant in town and am heating it up. We can cook the rest anytime you're ready. First, I thought we'd have a glass of wine."

Hailey hugged herself. This is the kind of evening she'd always imagined—a cozy time with a man she loved. She heard the howling wind and was glad the cabin was so snug.

She changed into her dry jeans and warm sweater and came back to the living room, content with life. Sitting on the couch with Nick, she couldn't stop staring at him. Though he was a handsome man, what she was really seeing was the happiness on his face. It made her feel good. She wondered what it would be like to have him sitting next to her on a couch every night. The idea was exciting.

He turned to her with a smile. "More wine?"

She held up her glass. "Thanks. On such a cold night, it makes me warm."

He rose to go to the kitchen.

Hailey watched him, admiring the view.

When he returned, he handed her the glass of wine and kissed her. She returned the kiss and wished it would always be this way between them.

At dinner, she noticed how at ease he was in the kitchen. "Have you always cooked? You seem like such a natural."

"Owning and running a candy store takes long hours. Mom made sure both Stacy and I were comfortable in the kitchen and able to start dinner for the three of us. I like it."

"Me, too," she said. "I'm not a fancy cook, but I make a mean salad."

He laughed. "After we finish here, I thought you might like to hear some music. I always need the practice."

"Sounds heavenly," she murmured. *Could he get any better?*

Later, she insisted on doing the dishes. While she was busy in the kitchen, Nick went to his keyboard and plugged it in. She heard the sound of scales being played, and curious, went to see.

"What are you doing?"

"Warming up. People might think I only play the

guitar, but I've been a piano player since I was a kid. Classical music and everything in between."

"Didn't you go away to study music?" she said.

"Yes. The Berklee College of Music in Boston. I got a great scholarship there."

"Wow! I didn't realize …"

His laughter stopped her. "No one could believe I gave that up to join a rock band. But a lot of rock musicians start out with classical training before they throw themselves into that kind of music." He went back to his warming-up routine.

She hurried into the kitchen to finish up the dishes, eager to see how else he might surprise her.

When she walked into the living room, he started playing. She sighed and clutched her hands. Debussy's "Girl With the Flaxen Hair" was a song she recognized from a college music appreciation class she'd taken. She lowered herself on the couch, leaned back, closed her eyes, and allowed the music to flow through her.

From Debussy to the musical theme of a recent movie, his music continued to soothe something inside her. She opened her eyes and smiled lazily at Nick. "I love hearing you play."

He grinned. "That makes all those hours of practice worthwhile."

She remembered feeling the same way when he'd talked about her books, and she studied him, seeing in him the kind of man she'd always hoped to have in her life.

A while later, when she couldn't stop yawning, she rose. "I'm ready for bed."

He played a quick riff on the keyboard and rose. "Me, too. First, I want to check the snow outside."

Hailey checked the window and followed him to the front door for a better view. Outside, the snow had stopped and a silence, prompted by white, soft flakes covering everything, greeted them.

"Oh," she whispered, "it's beautiful."

He wrapped an arm around her and drew her close. "It's moments like this when I know there's goodness in the world."

She nodded. She felt it too, the awe that comes from observing such sights.

They turned back, shut the door, and headed for bed.

The next morning when Hailey awoke, silence urged her to get out of bed and go to the window. The sun was rising in what promised to be a bright, blue sky. White snow crystals seemed to catch sunbeams, giving the entire scene a glittering light.

Nick came up behind her and placed a hand on her shoulder.

"Okay, it's time," he said.

"For what?" She turned to him with a questioning look.

He grinned. "Snow Angels!"

She laughed, delighted by the idea. "Really?"

He nodded. "It's one of Regan's favorite things to do. C'mon! It looks like fun out there."

"Okay, but while I get ready, can you please start the coffee? I think I'm going to need it."

He headed toward the kitchen, humming the song about Frosty. If possible, she liked him even more. He was just a kid at heart.

Later, when they'd both bundled up in coats, hats, gloves, and boots, Hailey headed outside feeling as overdressed as some of the toddlers in her wintertime story group.

She noticed a nice flat space between cabins and headed there, her boots plunging in and pulling out of the snow in tedious steps. When she reached the edge of the space she flopped down in the snow on her back and began moving her arms and legs, laughing when a small mound of it landed on her face. Sputtering, she sat up in time to see Nick making his own snow angel.

Bursting with love, she crawled over to him and kissed him.

He pulled her up on top of him and met her lips. "Hmmm, you're an angel."

When they finally pulled apart, Hailey rolled off him and sat up.

He got to his feet. "The snow is perfect for a snowman. Let's do it."

They set to work forming balls and rolling them around in the snow, stopping every so often to pack the snow.

"Looks like we've got the head to do," said Hailey as Nick stacked the two balls together.

"Get started. I'll be right back," said Nick.

She made another large ball and packed more snow around it. It was a perfect size when Nick emerged from the cabin carrying a hat and a scarf.

"I've got these," he said, waving them in the air.

They put the head atop the other two balls of snow and secured it.

Nick placed the hat on the head and wrapped the scarf around the snowman's neck.

Hailey studied it. "Nice, but what about his face?"

"Got it covered," Nick said, and pulled a carrot and some small stones from his pocket.

"These are great! Where'd you get the stones?"

He grinned. "From the potted plant in the living room. Figured Mr. Snowman needed these more than the plant. At least for the next few days."

At the sound of a chugging engine, they turned.

A small snow plow was clearing a path towards them.

Nick waved, and the man driving the plow stopped and idled the machine.

"Hey, Sam! How are things at the hotel?" Nick asked. "I'm technically on vacation from the maintenance department, but if I'm needed, I'll come to work."

The man shook his head. "Everything's fine. A few problems with some of the guests missing snow gear and all, but nothing serious. Enjoy yourself with your lady, Nick. Believe me, they'll call you if they need you. Ben is doing a great job of covering for you."

"Great! See you around." Nick grinned at Hailey. "Guess our playdate is still on."

Inside, Hailey pulled out her drawings, eager to get more ideas for the story that wouldn't stop playing in her head.

Nick brought her a cup of hot cocoa. "Let me see."

She leafed through her sketches. "These are just ideas that I'll refine later."

He pulled up a chair to the kitchen table and sat beside her while she talked about them.

"I don't know how you do that—come up with a story and draw the illustrations for it."

She shrugged. "It's not too different from what you do with music."

"Guess that makes us compatible," he said, winking at her.

"Yes, so I've learned," she said, pleased with how things were going.

"I have a question," he said, serious now. "How much of you is in Charlie?"

She sighed. "I've been asked that question before. The truth is probably a lot. He's a curious little boy who gets into trouble on his way to learning things about life. I'm a lot like that."

He cupped her face in his strong hands. "Do you think I'm trouble?"

"If you want to call it trouble, it's the best kind. And I'm learning a lot about life …" she hesitated, … "and about love."

His face lit with pleasure. He kissed her and then caressed her cheek. "I love you, Hailey."

Her eyes filled. "I know. I love you too."

The phone rang, startling them.

"I'll get it," said Nick rising.

Hailey hugged herself as she watched him pick up his cell, feeling as if this vacation was her imagination working overtime. Surely you couldn't fall in love with someone so quickly. But whatever she was feeling for Nick, she didn't want it to go away.

When Nick clicked off the call, he said, "Hope you don't mind, but I'm going to have to perform at the Granite Bar tonight. The group we contracted with to play can't make it because of the storm."

"Not a problem. It gives me another chance to see you play."

"Good. The Granite Rock Band will be behind me."

Hailey saw his excitement, and worry nipped at her like a pesky bug. "Nick? You told me you wanted to stay in Granite Ridge. But if you got the chance to tour again, would you do it?" She couldn't tell him how important his answer was to her.

He gave her a steady look. "If you're asking if I'm ready to go on tour anytime in the future, the answer is no. But I will want to continue my music with my local band, and I intend to do some teaching."

"Oh, okay," she said, unable to hide her relief. She'd never want to hold him back from doing what he wanted, but she wouldn't like it if he were gone all the time. Especially knowing what being on the road was really like for a lot of musicians.

That night, Hailey sat in the audience at a small table in the corner, feeling oddly nervous. Though Nick made it seem easy, singing on stage to an audience was something she knew she could never do.

Now, with Richie, Mike, and Chico and their instruments ready to go, she waited for Nick to arrive. A drum roll quieted the room and then loud rock music blared as Nick jumped up on stage, grabbed his guitar, and began to play.

The entire building seemed to sway to the beat of the loud music as the crowd within danced in place. The excitement in the air was contagious. Caught up in it, Hailey stood with the others and waved her hands back and forth in the air.

She was awed once again by the way Nick's hands and fingers flew over the strings of his guitar. When they stopped, the roar of the crowd was deafening. Hearing it, Hailey could well imagine how addictive it could be to be part of a group making music like that.

Nick came to the microphone. "The band and I

have been working on a slower, softer song and we'd like to play it for you now." He wiped at his forehead with a colorful red bandana. "Besides, we need a break."

The crowd laughed and settled down to hear the next song.

"Okay, here it is. 'Love Magic'."

The strands of music that followed were surprisingly lush compared to their earlier number. Couples stood and embraced and swayed to the music.

Nick's voice was pure and sweet as he sang the romantic words. It made her wish she were in his arms. He looked over at her and smiled, sending a shiver of emotions through her, making her feel treasured. A few people around her looked to see who he'd smiled at, then nodded a greeting to her.

The evening passed quickly as she immersed herself in the music. Watching Nick work the crowd, she understood why women flung themselves at him. He had a way of making people believe he was playing and singing just for them.

After their performance ended, many in the crowd left. Others stayed behind. Piped music played in the background as Nick and his band took care of their instruments.

Nick came over to her. "What did you think?"

"It was fantastic," she answered honestly.

"I've asked the guys to have a couple of beers with us. They've got a table for us in another part of the bar."

"Okay, sounds good." Hailey was thirsty, and a beer sounded good.

She followed Nick through the main room into a back room where a number of people were sitting at tables in front of a massive stone fireplace.

"It's a little quieter here, and I want you to meet the guys," Nick explained, holding a chair for her to take a seat at the table where the three other musicians sat.

He lowered himself into a chair next to her. "Hey, guys, this is Hailey Kirby. Hailey, meet Richie Duncan, Mike Greenly, and Chico Alvarez."

Smiling at her, the guys acknowledged her with nods of their heads, still sweaty and flushed from their performance.

"Hey, you're the library lady," said Chico. "My daughter Rose loves to come to story time."

"Rose is your daughter?" Hailey exclaimed. "She's adorable. I know your wife Jeannie, of course, and little Paco. It's very nice to meet you." Hailey studied the short stocky man with the long, black braid down his back and grinned. She loved his family.

"I hear you write books," said Richie Duncan. The drum player, an older man with graying hair at his temples, studied her.

"Yes," said Hailey. She glanced at Nick and back to Richie. "I write and illustrate picture books under my pen name, Lee Merriweather." Her hands, clutched in her lap, felt cold even as heat reached her cheeks. But, if she was going to "come out" so to speak, she wanted it to be with the townspeople she cared about.

Nick reached over and squeezed her hand.

"You write the Charlie stories?" said Chico. "Rose loves those books."

"Wow! That's cool," said Mike. "I hear Nick is doing some songs for that character named Charlie. How stellar is that? I've told him I'd be glad to help him with arrangements on the keyboard."

"That's so sweet," Hailey said. "What little I've heard has been terrific. I think the kids are really going to love them."

The rest of the evening went smoothly. Hailey enjoyed talking to the men in the band. They were nice guys, open and friendly. More importantly, by the time the gathering broke up, Hailey knew they all were in settled relationships, with spouses and children and no plans to do a lot of travel in far-away places. That meant Nick could enjoy his local band for some time.

Nick helped her into her coat, and they slipped out the door and headed for his cabin.

Outdoors, the moon was casting a golden glow on the snow, making it seem like a winter wonderland. Hailey had never really enjoyed winter that much, but she was discovering how beautiful it could be.

She glanced at Nick lugging his guitar. He caught her looking at him and grinned.

Sighing with contentment, she followed him inside the cozy cabin.

CHAPTER 12

The next morning when Hailey awoke, she lay in bed stretching languidly. It felt wonderful to be able to lie around with nothing to do. Between her job and her creative work, she was usually highly programmed.

Nick was singing in the shower. She lay still to listen for a few minutes, then climbed out of bed, wanting to surprise him with a hot breakfast.

In the kitchen, she fixed coffee and pulled a carton of eggs out of the refrigerator. She was debating what to make when Nick walked into the room.

"What's this?" he said, coming up to her and nuzzling her neck.

"I thought it was time I cooked for you," she said smiling at him.

"Okay. How about scrambled eggs and toast?"

"Coming up," Hailey said, glad he hadn't asked for anything fancy. She wasn't the best cook, but she was trying. She'd bought a lot of kitchen equipment when she'd moved into her condo, telling herself it was time to learn.

A short while later, she placed a plate of fluffy scrambled eggs and a slice of crispy, brown toast in front of Nick.

"Thanks." He took a bite and gave her a thumbs up. "Delicious."

"You're welcome," Hailey said, feeling ridiculously proud as she took a seat opposite him. "What shall we do today?"

"How about sledding? The hotel has a number of sleds we can use, and the hill has to be pretty well packed down by now."

Hailey grinned. "I haven't been on a sled in years."

"Well, then, it's about time you were. C'mon. Let's hurry and get dressed for the snow. It looks like a good morning, but I heard we might get some more winter weather later today."

Hailey took a final sip of coffee, carried her dishes over to the sink, and raced into the bedroom for a quick shower.

Later, dressed for the outdoors, she stepped outside. She lifted her face to the sky and inhaled the clean air, loving this opportunity to play with Nick. In the past several days, she'd learned more about the different sides to him and loved it all.

He took hold of her hand, and they headed to the top of the sledding hill, which was on the other side of the events building. They walked along the main road leading up to the ski areas that lay on the other side of the peak and turned off to go to a small wooden building where a number of sleds leaned up against the exterior walls. Kids and parents milled around as they waited for the all clear sign from below to take a turn.

The hill sloped gently, providing a long, steady ride. Hailey watched a number of people take off.

Soon it was their turn. Hailey climbed aboard the sled Nick held for her, and, sitting up, she took flight. She glanced back and saw Nick climb aboard another sled and then he, lying down on it, whizzed by her.

She picked up speed. Hailey's stomach twisted with fear then she began to laugh as the sled rose over a small bump and landed with a thud. Surprised, she held onto the rope and screamed with both fright and excitement as the sled gathered even more speed.

She flew past Nick and onto the hay spread out at the bottom of the hill to stop people from going any farther. Tossed onto her back, she stared up at the sky and laughed from deep in her belly. "Oh my God! That was so much fun!"

Nick sat beside her, laughing too. "You were flying, girl."

"I know," she said, laughing harder. "We'd better go again."

They dragged their sleds over to the road and began the climb up the mountain.

"Guess they don't have special lifts for this, huh?" Hailey said, tugging on her sled.

"No, ma'am. I think parents like the idea of making the kids work for another run down the hill."

"Yes, I can see that," said Hailey, feeling the muscles in her legs work hard.

After three more runs, Hailey announced, "I'm ready for a break."

"Me, too," Nick admitted. He gave her a sheepish look. "I'm hungry too."

"All right. Let's pick up some sandwiches from the snack shop and head back to your cabin. I just thought of a couple of things I want to add to the Christmas story. Charlie definitely has to go sledding."

"Deal," said Nick. "I need to check in with the office to make sure I'm not needed."

"I might run up to my room and pick up a couple of things," Hailey said. "I'll meet you in the lobby."

Hailey checked the lobby to see if anyone in her family was there, but no Kirby woman was around. She took the elevator to her room thinking how strange it was that she'd hardly seen her family this vacation, but it still felt right. They were busy, social women who, no doubt, needed this break as much as she.

In her room, she grabbed some fresh clothes and put them in the plastic laundry bag the hotel had provided. After she checked to make sure everything was in order, she closed the door behind her.

Nick had already purchased some food when she met up with him in the lobby. He said goodbye to the woman behind the activities desk and they walked outside. Hailey thought she saw her mother in the distance but kept on walking. She wasn't quite ready to have Nick officially meet her mother even though Mom already knew Hailey was totally in love with him.

They'd just finished lunch in the cabin when Nick's cell rang. He checked caller ID and frowned.

"Hey, Stacy. What's up?"

Hailey watched with alarm as his face drained of color. "Oh, my God! Is she going to be all right? Granite Ridge Regional? Okay, I'll meet you there. Oh? Okay, I'll ask Hailey to come too."

Hailey jumped to her feet. "What's wrong?"

"Regan has been hurt. Apparently, a car lost control in the snow and skidded up onto the sidewalk in front of the store where Regan was playing. She's at Granite Ridge Regional Hospital."

"Oh my God!" Hailey's heart skipped a beat. She closed her eyes to stop the room from spinning and opened them to steady herself. "Is she going to be all right?"

Nick bowed his head and shook it. "I don't know."

She took hold of his arm. "Come, let's go! I'll drive."

She grabbed her purse and put on her coat, keeping a steady eye on Nick. He looked as if his insides had disappeared, leaving him limp as a rag doll.

"Better call the bellmen's station and ask them to bring the car around," said Nick. "If we're lucky, it'll be there waiting for us."

She made the call while Nick looked around for his wallet and moments later, they left the cabin for the walk back to the hotel.

"What else did Stacy tell you?" Hailey gently asked.

"Regan was semi-conscious when the ambulance arrived. They don't know what damage she sustained. They're assessing her now. Stacy was crying so hard I could hardly understand her."

"Poor thing." Her vision blurred. Of all the children who came to story time, Regan was always one of the most excited.

At the hotel, they had to wait only a few minutes for Hailey's car to be brought to the front.

Hailey slid behind the wheel while Nick climbed into the passenger seat. Glancing at him, she was glad he'd allowed her to drive. He looked a wreck.

On the road winding down to the valley, they were quiet. Hailey's thoughts whirled inside her head. Though Regan was a delicately boned child, she had a strong nature. The thought of any permanent damage was nauseating. No wonder Nick was so upset.

Hailey entered the edge of town and turned right. Granite Ridge Regional Hospital had not been established merely for skiers and outdoorsmen in the area.

Outside of Boise and other big cities in Idaho, it was the largest of its kind, filled with the best of equipment and highly qualified medical personnel with specialized training. For exceptional cases, medical centers in Boise and Salt Lake City were available.

As they drew closer to the hospital, the tension in the car grew stronger.

Hailey reached over and took hold of Nick's hand. "It's going to be all right."

"I hope so," he murmured. "I feel like Regan is mine. You know?"

She nodded. "I do. You're so good with her."

Hailey dropped him off at the Emergency entrance and parked the car. As she rushed inside, she whispered a prayer that all would be well.

The woman behind the registration desk looked up at her. "Are you Hailey Kirby?"

"Yes. I'm here for Regan ..."

The woman stood. "Come with me."

Heart pounding, Hailey followed her into a large room where beds, curtained off for privacy, were lined up. She heard Nick's deep voice and hurried to it. The partially open curtain allowed her a glimpse of the bed where Regan lay. Her eyes were closed.

"Is she in a coma?" Hailey whispered as she hugged Stacy.

"No, she's sleeping now. They gave her a sedative so they could set a broken bone in her arm. They're coming to get her for a CT Scan to check for any internal injuries." Stacy's face drained of color as tears streamed down her cheeks. "I didn't see Regan sneak out the door of the shop. I should have kept a better eye on her, but my New Year's rush orders are keeping me busy."

"It wouldn't have happened if I'd been there to watch her," said Nick with a grim expression. "I was wrong to take vacation at such a busy time of year." He avoided looking at Hailey.

Hailey bit her lip, holding in a cry. *Was Nick sorry he'd spent this time with her?*

Stacy noticed her reaction and understood. She turned to him. "No, Nick. I don't want you to feel that way. I know how much the last several days have meant to you. Don't ruin it by thinking like this."

Nick studied Hailey, and nodded. "You're right, sis. These past few days with Hailey have been the best of my life."

Hailey's smile was wobbly. He'd had the chance to break her heart.

A doctor followed by an aide walked up to them. "Okay, we're all set for the CT Scan. This aide will take her there. I suggest you go to the waiting area in the pediatric ward to await word from us there. As we've already told you, her blood work looks good. But with a child this small, we don't take any chances on missing something. So far, in addition to the small fracture in her forearm, we've found a few contusions, but nothing very serious as far as we can tell. Thanks to heavy winter wear, it could've been worse. I'm sure they were a big protection factor for her."

After the doctor left, Nick turned to Stacy. "Tell me exactly what happened to Regan."

"I didn't see all of it, of course," Stacy said. "By the time I realized what was happening and ran outside, Regan was on the ground on her back. A car was barely over the edge of the curb. A woman was standing beside it yelling for help."

"Were there witnesses?" Hailey asked.

"Oh, yes!" Stacy said. "Mabel Jenkins came rushing out of the café right after it happened. She told me she saw it. The car came up over the curb at the same time Regan was chasing after her new rubber ball. The car wasn't going fast, just slowly sliding forward, but the front bumper hit Regan squarely."

"Dammit! I gave Regan the ball. I told her it was for outdoors, not indoors. That must be why she took it outside," Nick pulled a hand through his hair.

"Nick, it was an accident," said Hailey, taking hold of his free hand. "One of those awful accidents that sometimes happen out of the blue."

"Hailey's right," said Stacy. "We can blame ourselves over and over again, but it won't help anything. What we need to do now is make sure Regan is all right."

"Yes, of course." He gave Stacy a weak smile. "How'd you get so smart?"

"Let's go upstairs to the pediatric ward." Stacy turned to Hailey. "You too. It will mean so much to Regan if she sees you." Her lips quivered. "Maybe you'd even read to her, like she enjoys."

"I'd be glad to," said Hailey. "I'll read one of my books to her."

"Your books?"

"I'm Lee Merriweather," Hailey said simply, remembering her conversation with Stacy earlier, the one in which Stacy had told her Nick seemed to be in love with Lee Merriweather.

Stacy's jaw dropped. "Well, I'll be! No wonder Nick is love struck."

Hailey and Nick glanced at one another. Nick put his arm around Hailey's waist and kissed her cheek.

"Well, then, it's about time you found each other 'cause I think you're perfect together," said Stacy with a nod of approval.

CHAPTER 13

They took the elevator to the third floor and walked into the pediatric wing. Though no one else was in the waiting room, Hailey took a seat next to Stacy. Nick said he couldn't sit still and began to pace the room.

Hailey was at the point of asking Nick to please stop pacing when the doctor appeared. "We've had the chance to get a better look at Regan. It appears her spleen is bruised, which means she's going to have a very tender spot on her upper left abdomen for a while. But it should heal by itself in time. No sign of broken ribs or any other concerns. We figure she used her arm to protect herself."

"Thank you, Doctor. Thank you so much! Where is she now?" Stacy asked, her voice quivery. "Is she awake?"

"She's groggy but awake. She's just being brought up now." He smiled at them. "Such a bright little girl.

She's got a whole list of people she wants to see. Who's Charlie?"

Stacy and Nick turned to her.

"He's a character in one of my books. Regan's one of my regulars at story time," Hailey said. It felt good to be able to talk about her books without insecurities holding her back. Jo had tried to talk to her about it, but Nick was the person who'd helped her understand it was worth it to put her own name behind her work. He'd shown her by example. She knew him well enough to sense how nervous he was before a performance, but he did it anyway.

"Well, with you, Nick, and Regan's mother, it seems to me Regan's going to have a good recovery. We'll keep her overnight, and then she can go home to rest." He gave them an encouraging nod and left the waiting area.

After Stacy left to check in with the nurse's station, Hailey turned to Nick. "I'll do anything I can to help, even if it includes working in the candy store."

"Right! I forgot about that part. Okay, we'll check in with Stacy and Regan, and then, if necessary, we can all take turns at the store. I happen to know that the lodge placed a huge order for New Year's Eve. I'm sure other businesses and people did too. It's sort of a tradition here in town."

Hailey and Nick waited in the hallway to give Stacy a few minutes alone with Regan when she was brought to her room.

"Okay," Nick said. "I can't wait any longer." He

knocked gently on the door and entered the private room, Hailey at his heels.

"Hey, Regan. It's Uncle Nick," he said quietly, approaching the bed.

"Hi, Unca Nick," said Regan, smiling sleepily and holding out her arms to him. She winced.

"Hold on there, Regan. Better to lie still." He bent over the side bars on the bed and kissed her cheek. "Guess who I brought with me?"

"Charlie?"

"Better than that. Charlie's mommy, Miss Kirby."

The smile that spread across Regan's face warmed Hailey's heart. She was such an adorable little girl. "Hi, Regan," she said softly, taking hold of the little girl's hand and squeezing it. "Later, when you get more rest, I'll come and read Charlie stories to you. How about that?"

"Okay," Regan said, her eyes beginning to close.

The three of them stood and watched for a few minutes.

"I'm so relieved she's going to be fine," said Stacy.

"Hailey has offered to help at the store," Nick said to Stacy. "Why don't I stay with Regan while you show Hailey what to do? Then, when you come back, I'll go help too. We can all take turns."

"We can pick up Regan's books too," offered Hailey.

"Good idea. Mabel is watching the store for me, but she needs to be at the café." Stacy leaned over and gave Regan another kiss, then turned to Hailey. "Let's go, so I can hurry back."

Hailey blew a kiss to Nick and left the room.

From the moment she'd first walked inside the store years ago with Mom, Hensley's Sweet Shoppe held a sense of magic for Hailey. It wasn't just the delicious aromas or the bright colors that filled the space, but the rows and rows of fine chocolates sitting behind glass waiting to become someone's treat.

Filled with that memory, Hailey turned to Stacy. "Did you know I learned to read a lot of words here in the shop? My sisters used to help me read all your signs for candy."

Stacy chuckled. "Do you mean hard words like coconut, nougat and the like?"

"Exactly. I was fascinated with everything. Wanted to taste it all. I don't know how you stay so thin working here in the store."

"Believe me, you get used to it. Sure, I nibble now and then, but I don't gobble down too many at a time. But you, Hailey, may have as many bites as you want while working here."

"Thanks. I'll try to be good, but it sure is tempting."

Mabel Jenkins came from the back of the store and greeted them. "How's Regan? I've been so worried about her."

"She's going to be all right," said Stacy, receiving a hug from Mabel.

Hailey observed them with affection. Gray-haired, sweet Mabel, wearing the Christmas apron she never seemed to take off, was a valued member of the community. She and her husband Rusty ran the café in town, supported local youth baseball and soccer teams, and were the stand-in grandparents for a lot of kids who knew where to find a free cookie now and then.

Mabel turned to her now. "How are you, Hailey? I hear the kids at the library are missing you."

"I'm fine, thank you. Enjoying my vacation at the lodge with my family."

"I hear sweet Alissa and her man are married now. Such a shame to put her through such an emotional roller coaster and then up and marry her."

"We're all very happy about it," said Hailey, coming to their defense. Jed was a nice guy whom Alissa adored.

"While you two chat, I'll go get the Charlie books," said Stacy. She grinned at Mabel. "Did you know Hailey is the author of those stories? She writes them under the pen name of Lee Merriweather."

Mabel's eyes widened. "Oh, my stars! Wait until Helen Chadwick hears this! She'll have to put a huge display of them at the bookstore."

"Maybe the news will finally put a smile on that frowny face of hers," said Stacy.

"Or not," said Hailey. Helen Chadwick was a disagreeable woman who owned and ran the bookstore, a valuable part of the town. Only trouble was, she was a book snob who thought she knew everything there was about publishing books. Her behavior was one reason Hailey had never pushed to have her books in the store. Fortunately, Helen liked them enough to do it on her own.

"Well, she does have pride in Granite Ridge. I'll speak to her about it," said Mabel, volunteering to act as the go-between as usual.

Stacy left, and Mabel led Hailey to the cash register. "This one is a lot simpler than the register we have at the café. Let me show you."

Hailey listened and made notes as Mabel led her through the procedure. It was a machine that recorded inventory as well, so entering the right SKU number was important. A list of those numbers for each item was covered in plastic and posted next to the cash register. Otherwise, it was a simple operation.

Stacy returned. "Okay, thank you, Mabel. I know you have to get back to the café, but I appreciate your help so much. Want to take some chocolates with you?"

Mabel shook her head and patted her ample stomach. "No, thanks. I had a few while you were gone."

Hailey and Stacy glanced at one another and laughed. "No worries. I told Hailey it was all right to do the same thing," Stacy said.

After Mabel left, Stacy took Hailey into the back and showed her how to package up the chocolate orders that were ready. "With the Winterfest celebration still going on, people will dribble in and out all day. But I really need this packaging done. Maybe tomorrow you can help me in the kitchen."

"Sure. Any way I can help. I also want to read to Regan."

"Of course." Stacy fluttered her hands in front of her. "And you need to spend time with Nick. I don't want to do anything to interfere with that. I've never seen him so happy."

"Thanks, Stacy, but we both love Regan and want to be here for you."

"Like I said, you two are perfect for one another. If only my mother were here to see the two of you together." Stacy's smile was wicked. "Hot, hot, hot!"

Hailey's cheeks turned pink. That's exactly how she thought of Nick.

After Stacy left. Hailey decided to call Mom to let her know what happened. She punched in Mom's number on her cell and waited for her to pick up. Her message memo came on. Frowning at the idea that it had been a while since they'd connected, Hailey left a message telling her mother about Regan's accident and that she'd left the hotel to help Stacy and probably wouldn't return for a day or two.

She clicked off the call, well aware that once again no mention was made of Nick. The entire family would find out soon enough how she felt about him.

Hailey was in the back in the kitchen when she heard a customer come in. She set aside the chocolates she'd been working with, removed the plastic gloves she'd been told she had to wear when handling them, and headed to the front.

Helen Chadwick stood there looking like she was about to explode. A retired school teacher in her late sixties, she was, as always, impeccably dressed in a black skirt, a white blouse, and gray sweater. Her face was pinched with anger.

Hailey's stomach plummeted. "Hi, Mrs. Chadwick. What can I help you with?"

"You may, not can, help me by telling me exactly why you'd exclude a certain detail about the children's books that have become so popular."

"I … I…"

"To think you're actually Lee Merriweather! As the bookstore owner in town, I should have been accorded the courtesy of knowing that. Where are your manners, girl?"

Hailey looked down and let out a sigh. Mrs. Chadwick had always intimidated her. Gaining a breath, she lifted her head. "No one but my family knew. That's how I wanted it. I had to be sure I wouldn't become the laughingstock of people who would judge me harshly. I've recently decided to let people know what I do. Of course, I'd tell you, but I haven't had the chance to do so."

"Well," said Mrs. Chadwick, a bit mollified. "You were always shy, barely spoke in class, but your writing spoke volumes. They are endearing books. I expect you to sign some for me and to hold a party at the book store."

"Of course. I'd be honored. I have to be in touch with my agent and editor to get some books for you. But we'll come up with a plan."

"Thank you, Hailey. I remember you as one of my most promising students in English. I'm glad to see you enjoy success."

Hailey's clamped her jaw to keep it from dropping. Helen Chadwick did not give out compliments lightly.

"Thank you, Mrs. Chadwick. That means the world to me."

She nodded briskly, turned, and left the store as new customers came in.

Watching her go, Hailey couldn't help the smile that spread across her face. Maybe being known as Lee Merriweather wouldn't be difficult, after all.

She was busy with customers when Nick walked into the store. She looked up at him and smiled. He looked … well … delicious.

After the store had closed, Hailey and Nick worked together packaging chocolates.

Stacy called to say Regan was sleeping soundly and she'd like them to come to the hospital so she could make more candy.

"Why don't you head over?" Nick suggested. "I'll

meet you there. I need to make sure Stacy will be okay. She needs to get some sleep."

"I promised to help her in the morning," said Hailey. "But you're right. I don't like the idea of her staying up all night making candy. She needs her rest if she's going to care for Regan.

Nick gave her a smile that made her heart race. "You're such a good person, Hailey. Know that?" He came over to her and hugged her. "I'm so glad I found you."

His lips met hers, and she responded, loving the feel of them, the taste of them.

After Stacy left Regan's hospital room, Hailey sat next to the bed and lifted the sleeping child's hand in her own, sending prayers for her to be strong and get well soon. She'd always wanted a lot of children of her own and at least one adopted child. Seeing Regan like this, she wondered if she'd be as strong, as capable a mother as Stacy. Mom was a role model she'd always looked up to. Now, Stacy was another.

Her thoughts drifted to Nick. He'd already proved to her what a great father he'd be. How would he feel about children of his own?

As if her thoughts had attracted him, he appeared.

"How are things going?" he asked softly. He gave her a kiss on the cheek and pulled up a chair next to hers.

"She's sleeping. I'm sure her little body is trying to heal, so all this sleep is good for her."

Regan stirred, moaned, and opened her eyes. When she saw them, she smiled and her eyes brightened. "Read to me?"

"Of course, Regan," said Hailey. She opened the book about Charlie running away and began to read, acting out the characters with different voices.

Nick sat back in his chair, listening to her.

As she neared the end of the book, she read:

"Charlie's mother hugged him tight. 'I'm so glad you came home. I missed you."

'I promise not to run away again,' said Charlie. He hadn't been gone long. After going only one block, with his dachshund, Zeke, he wished he hadn't done it. Like his mother had told him, 'Home is where the heart is' and he knew his home was with her and the rest of his family.

The End"

"I'm glad Charlie went home," Regan said, as she always did at the end of this book.

"I am too," Hailey said, caressing Regan's cheek.

Regan tried to sit up, moaned and lay back against her pillow. "I want to go home!" she cried.

"Hey, monkey! You're going to go home tomorrow. I'm going to stay right here with you until then. How about I sing you a couple of songs?"

"Okay," Regan said, her eyes beginning to droop once more.

Nick's soft voice was sweet as he sang one song after another Hailey recognized from a children's songbook the library carried.

She listened, captivated by the sound of it. Nick was such a contradiction to the man people saw play in a rock band—the confident, glitzy star who didn't seem to have a care in the world but what song was up next. This person softly singing his heart out for his injured niece was the one she loved best.

When Regan was sleeping soundly again and all was quiet in the room, Hailey lifted his hand and kissed it.

"What was that for?" Nick asked, smiling.

"For being you. That's all."

"Thanks," he said. "And thanks for being here. It means a lot."

"I'm glad I can help."

"Stacy told me she blabbed to Mabel about your being Lee Merriweather. Are you mad about it?"

"No," Hailey replied with a firmness she felt to her toes. "It's past time that it all came out. As scary as it can be to have so many people judging me, I owe my readers, or I should say the parents of my readers, honesty. I'm not going to hide anymore."

"I like that," said Nick. "When someone like you puts herself out there, she has to understand that others can choose to admire what she does or not. Any cruelty that accompanies it needs to be ignored because nobody can take what you do and make it exactly like yours."

"Spoken by someone in the public eye," teased Hailey.

He grinned. "Yeah, I've had to tell myself that a time or two."

"Thank you for sharing that with me. It means a lot."

"Look, I'm going to stay here. If you're going to help Stacy in the morning, why don't you go home and get some rest?"

"Good idea. This has been an exhausting day, and I promised I'd be there to help." She got to her feet.

Nick stood and drew her to him in a hug that almost crushed her. "Thanks for being you," he said, repeating her earlier words to him.

CHAPTER 14

After being with Nick for the last couple of nights, it felt strange for Hailey to be back in her condo and alone. But as she crawled into bed, she was grateful for the opportunity to get a good night's sleep. Working in the candy store wasn't as easy as she'd thought. Another reason to admire Stacy.

What seemed a short time later, Hailey awoke to the sound of her alarm blaring. For a moment, she thought it was a regular workday at the library. Then it all came back—the time at the lodge, being with Nick, and Regan's accident. She turned off the alarm and got out of bed, determined to be there for Stacy.

After a shower and dressing, Hailey went into the kitchen for her morning coffee. Inhaling the aroma of the hot liquid in her cup, she let out a grateful sigh. She stared out the window at the mountain and the lodge. What had always been beautiful to her now held much more meaning after her time there with Nick.

She wondered where their relationship would go from here. She knew how they felt about one another, but would they decide to slow down, see where time took them? One thing she knew for certain, she loved him and didn't want to face being left behind. The thought of losing him brought back her childhood fear of not being good enough.

She checked the time and grabbed a granola bar. She'd eat it on the way to the store.

Driving through town she reminded herself to take a little time to enjoy the Winterfest that was still going on. Though the main festival took place before Christmas, the stores and businesses along Main Street continued to hold special events through New Year's Eve. Not quite as festive, but it was still fun.

Hailey pulled her car in behind the Sweet Shoppe, got out, and knocked on the door.

Stacy opened it and waved her inside. "We just got another big order for Christmas Kisses. I've made the caramels but they all need to be wrapped. There are a few left of the special order of chocolate-covered caramels that need to be dipped and set aside."

"Okay. I'll do my best. You look exhausted. How late did you stay up?"

"Too late. I can barely see I'm so tired."

"You go ahead upstairs to sleep. I'll take care of everything," said Hailey. It couldn't be too hard to handle the store for a few hours, could it?

Hailey was at work wrapping caramels in bright silver foil when she heard a knock at the door. She checked her watch and frowned. The store wasn't due to open for another half-hour.

She went to the front door, flipped on the lights and, seeing the mayor of the town, opened the door. "Hello, Mayor. What can I do for you?"

Elizabeth Goode clutched her hands and gave her a pleading look. "Is there any way I can buy a box of chocolates? I'm having a staff meeting and thought they all deserved a treat after dealing with the snow storm."

"Of course, you can," Hailey said, waving her inside.

"By the way, how is little Regan? I heard all about the accident."

"She's going to be fine. Poor thing has a broken arm and a bruised spleen. She'll need to take it easy for a while. That will be the hard part for Stacy."

"It's horrifying when something like this happens. I understand the driver was from out of town and wasn't used to driving in snowy weather. But I also learned that Regan was running toward the street to get the ball. I suppose there will be no charges."

"That hasn't been mentioned at all," said Hailey, going behind the counter. "Now, which chocolates would you like boxed up?"

Hailey waited patiently while Elizabeth chose

twelve different chocolates, then slowly rang them up, realizing too late she'd mixed up a few flavors in the cash register. She went ahead and rang up the charge, telling herself she'd make a note of the changes. Cocoa and coconut were a little confusing on the list when she was trying to hurry.

She'd just finished putting a holiday ribbon around the box of chocolates when another customer entered the store.

She said goodbye to Elizabeth and greeted the new customer.

After helping her to a special holiday box of assorted chocolates, she rang up the sale and hurried to the back to continue wrapping caramels. When she saw the ones set aside to be dipped into chocolate she hesitated and then, putting on her gloves, she tried dipping one into the chocolate Stacy had left in a warming pot. After making sure it was completely covered, she placed it on the waxed paper to the side. It looked fine, but it had taken longer than she'd hoped. She set those aside and went back to wrapping the caramels.

Another customer came in, and Hailey left her work in the back to help a man she recognized from the library. They exchanged greetings, and she quickly rang up the items he picked out.

Stacy stuck her head into the shop. "I'm on my way to the hospital to pick up Regan. Thanks, Hailey."

Hailey was finishing up another customer when Nick showed up. He waited until she was through ringing up the sale and said, "Need a little help? You look a little flustered." He kissed her.

"I want to get all the caramels wrapped and some others dipped in chocolate. If you help the customers, I can keep going in the back." She shook her head. "I don't know how Stacy does it."

"Practice, practice, practice," he said, grinning. "I'll dip the caramels in chocolate until a customer comes. How about that?"

"You know how to do it?" she said, surprised.

"It's a family business, remember?" he teased. "I know how to make a lot of the stuff."

"Okay, then. Dipping is yours. I'll do the rest of wrapping. Tell me. How is Regan doing?"

"When I left her, she was awake and waiting for Stacy to show up. It's going to be hard to keep her quiet. Even so, she's sore."

"I'll try to read to her a little later, after she gets settled at home and Stacy gets some more rest."

Standing in the back, working together, Hailey discreetly watched Nick work. True to his word, he knew exactly how to hand-dip chocolates.

She established a pattern to her work and was soon speeding along with her task. While they worked, she told him about the conversation with the mayor.

"There won't be any legal action on our part," said Nick. "As you said earlier, it was an accident. An accident I wish had never happened."

"I wonder how some mothers do it with a lot of kids," commented Hailey.

"How many kids do you want?" Nick asked.

"I've always wanted at least three of my own. And I want to adopt at least one."

Nick's eyebrows shot up. "So, you're talking four kids minimum? That's a handful."

"Mom did well with the four of us girls."

"Are you talking about wanting all girls?" he asked, giving her a look of dismay.

"I would take what I was given, both girls and boys. Why?"

He shrugged. "Just thinking."

"When I have a family, I also want to have dogs. That's one thing Mom did for us right after we arrived at her house. I had my stuffed dog, Charlie, but we had live dogs from the beginning. I think all kids should have pets, especially dogs, in their lives."

"I agree. Because of the shop, I couldn't have a dog, but I love them."

Their conversation was interrupted by Stacy. "Hey, Nick, help me carry Regan upstairs, will you?"

"Sure." They both went outside to Stacy's car where Regan was carefully buckled into her car seat in the back.

Hailey waved to her.

Regan waved back as Nick got her out of the seat and carefully held her in his arms.

"Can you read me a story?" Regan asked her.

"Yes, a little later," Hailey replied, relieved to see Regan so alert.

She waited until Nick had gone inside and was

headed upstairs with Regan before hurrying back to the store.

When Nick returned, he grinned at her. "Things seemed to be settled down. Mind if I take some time and go to the hotel? I need to check in there. Stacy's napping now. She said to tell you she'll relieve you later this morning."

"Not a problem. Go, check in, and, Nick, get some rest yourself. You look exhausted."

"Thanks." He pulled her into his arms. "What would we do without you?" he murmured. His warm breath in her ear sent a tingle of excitement through her.

She hugged him tightly, hardly able to get her arms around his solid, strong body.

After he left, Hailey finished up in the back room, put it in order and went to the front of the store. It was quiet now, but Hailey knew it wouldn't last. People from out of town were still arriving to visit Granite Ridge. And why wouldn't they? It was the picture-perfect image of a Christmas village with snow-covered roofs, banners hanging across the street, and decorations on the doors and in the windows of shops and businesses. She loved her town.

Mabel Jenkins arrived. "Hey, there! I just wanted to check on Regan. How is she?"

Hailey filled her in. "Stacy is going to need help

for the next day or two until she works out a routine with Regan."

"Don't forget. Madison Avery is available for babysitting while she's home from college. She can use the money."

"Good idea," said Hailey, jotting down a note for Stacy.

A sly smiled crossed Mabel's face. "Have you seen the display in the bookstore. All your Charlie books are being featured and Helen included a photo of you. I don't know what you said to her, but she's going all out for you."

Hailey laughed. "She was annoyed I didn't confide in her. But she'll make good use of the information, which is great. I haven't had the chance to tell my agent or editor yet, but they'll be thrilled."

"Good for you. Well, 'gotta go. Say hi to Stacy and tell her Rusty and I are here if she needs us."

Hailey smiled as Mabel hurried out of the store. No doubt she'd make sure that everyone knew who Lee Merriweather was. It was all part of living in a small town.

CHAPTER 15

That evening, Hailey stayed with Regan while Stacy met friends for a dinner that had been planned for a long time. After experiencing how tied down Stacy must feel working the store, Hailey understood the need for her to get out on her own.

Regan was excited to have Hailey to herself, clinging to her hand as Hailey sat and read to her.

They were in the middle of the book about saying good night to the moon when Nick appeared. "Ah, here are two of my three favorite girls." He kissed Hailey on the lips and bent down to give Regan a kiss on the cheek. "How are you feeling, monkey?"

"I gots a cast. See?" She held up her arm to him again to show him the pink cast covering her forearm.

"You're a brave girl," Nick said.

"We're doing better," said Hailey, indicating

Regan with a nod of her head. "We're learning how to lie still. Right, Regan?"

Regan nodded. "It's hard, Unca Nick."

His lips curved into an indulgent smile. "I bet Charlie would be proud of you for trying."

"Charlie might end up with a broken bone too someday," said Hailey to him quietly, her imagination already conjuring up some of the story.

"A true storyteller," Nick said, winking at her. "Always thinking."

"I can't help it," she said. "He's such a dear character."

Regan gazed at them. "Can Charlie get another dog? A dog like Zeke?"

"Oh, that would be lovely," said Hailey. "I'll try to work it out. How about that?"

Regan nodded. "Yes. He wants one. A puppy."

"We'll see," said Hailey, liking the idea.

A short while later, Stacy appeared at the apartment looking happy and relaxed. "Madison Avery called me back. She's pleased to be able to work for me for the next couple of weeks. It's such a relief."

"I've always heard nice things about her," said Hailey. "I'm glad you'll have extra help. When can she start?"

"The day after tomorrow, on New Year's Eve. Her boyfriend lives out of town and isn't going to be here for that, so she's happy to have something to do."

"Okay, I'll help out tomorrow then," said Hailey. "Maybe I'll get a little better working with those candy kisses and chocolates."

"That's a deal. If you work in the store, I'll take care of a few office matters while watching Regan." Stacy embraced her. "You're such a doll. I'm glad you and Nick are together."

Hailey felt the smile that spread her lips and nodded. "Me too." She glanced over at him. A tender expression had softened his classic features.

"Yeah, me too," he growled playfully. "C'mon, Hailey. Let's go. I haven't seen your condo yet."

Hailey was relieved he didn't wiggle his eyebrows at her. The sexy look he gave her was enough to spread a knowing look across Stacy's face.

Hailey pulled up to her building eager to show off her condo to Nick. Hers was an end unit on the second floor, which she loved, one of eight condos in an attractive, two-story, gray-clapboard structure with sparkling white trim.

"Nice," said Nick, getting out of the car. "I decided to rent an apartment in town until I got my situation with my agent settled. Now, with most of my money back, my accountant says I need to buy or build a house for financial reasons. I haven't decided what I want to do."

"I love my condo. It's so right for me," Hailey said. "Wait until you see it."

"If you like it, I'm sure I will too." He got out of the car and waited for her, then followed her inside and up the stairs to her door.

She unlocked it and, grinning, waved him inside. "Here it is. All mine."

He stood in the entry and looked around. "Cool. I like how you've decorated it."

Hailey had kept the walls a warm cream. Most of the furniture was upholstered in gray tones, but she'd popped color in the room with bright patterned pillows and colorful, modern artwork on the walls. The look was both comfortable and sophisticated.

"This is what I like best." She led him to the picture window that looked out to the mountain. In the dark, they saw the lights of the lodge way up high, twinkling at them. "In daylight, the view is spectacular."

"Pretty spectacular now," he murmured standing behind her and encircling her waist with his arms. "So are you," he murmured, nuzzling her neck.

Shivers of pleasure shot through her. She turned around and lifted her arms, meeting his lips with hers.

When they broke apart, Hailey studied him, seeing the pleasure in his eyes. How, she wondered, could it be possible to fall in love so quickly, so deeply? But it was true. She loved him in a way she'd never loved anyone else.

"If you want, look around while I see what we have to eat. I don't know about you, but I'm hungry. I didn't really eat dinner, just nibbled on a few things Stacy offered."

"I'm always up for a snack," said Nick, following her into the kitchen.

She opened the refrigerator. "How about a cheese omelet? I can make a green salad to go with it."

"Sounds good. I'm happy to help with the omelet."

"Okay. I'll do the salad."

She found once again that they worked well together. And later, when they made love, she found it was delightfully true too.

Hailey awoke with a start when she saw the outline of Nick beside her and then filled with warmth at the memory of the generous way that he'd made love, pleasing her.

She checked her watch, surprised to see how late it was. "Nick, I have to get up. I'm going to be late to help Stacy."

He groaned and rolled over. "Already?"

"Yes. This is my last day to help Stacy for a while, and I want to be there for her." She jumped out of bed and headed into the bathroom.

When she returned, he was still in bed. She grinned. "C'mon, lazybones, time to get up."

He opened his eyes. "Since when did you become so mean?"

Chuckling, she replied, "Since I began helping

your sister. I'll make coffee in the kitchen. Meet you there."

She paused while he climbed out of bed, and then she headed to the kitchen. She was sipping coffee, letting her thoughts wander, when Nick strolled in, his hair still wet from a quick shower.

"Mmm, smells good. And cinnamon toast? Wow! I haven't had that since I was a kid."

"Every once in a while, I treat myself," she said, remembering many childhood mornings when she'd had such a treat as a reward for eating a healthier breakfast.

Nick sipped his coffee between bites of the toast. "I'm going to the hotel today. My vacation is over."

"I have a favor to ask. Will you come to the New Year's Eve party at the lodge with me? My family will all be there, and I want you to be my guest."

"I'll make sure of it, even if I might be called away from time to time." He studied her. "Are you ready to tell them about us? Because when I'm with you, I can't hide my feelings."

"I want them all to know how happy I am when I'm with you," said Hailey. She'd hardly seen her family. This would be the perfect way for them to understand why.

They finished their coffee and then they took off —Nick to go to the lodge, and Hailey to spend another day at the candy store, learning all about making chocolates and other sweet treats.

❄

By day's end, Hailey was exhausted. She was used to working, but standing on the tile floor in the kitchen and in the store behind the cash register was hard on her feet. Stacy worked with her when she could, but she mostly stayed in her office where she'd set up a place for Regan to play quietly and rest.

That night, alone in her bed, Hailey missed Nick. He made her so happy with his easy-going manner, the different ways he made her smile. Was she ready for him to meet her family?

The answer was a resounding "yes!"

CHAPTER 16

Hailey left the town and headed toward the lodge with a sense of anticipation. The vacation had been full of surprises—from Alissa's on-again wedding to meeting Nick and falling in love. She could hardly wait to share everything with her family.

Smiling, she thought of how each woman in the family was independent, yet how close they were. She'd missed some of that closeness as they all did their own thing on this vacation. Maybe having Alissa married was part of it, but it seemed to her that life was changing dramatically for all of them.

She drove up to the front of the hotel feeling as if she'd been away for months, not three days.

Back in her room at the hotel, Hailey gazed around the suite and took a moment to pull herself together. It had been an emotional couple of days. The memory of Regan lying in bed helpless and fragile, wouldn't leave her mind. They were so lucky she was all right. Hailey thought of how fragile life itself was and vowed that going forward, she wouldn't be afraid to embrace anything life had to offer.

Tonight, she was celebrating New Year's Eve with her family. She'd use this special time to show them how much Nick meant to her. They already knew him in a neighborly way, but not as the man she loved with all her heart. The thought of surprising them with this news brought a smile to her face.

Though he had to work at the hotel, Nick had promised to escort her to the party, even if they got off to a late start. He'd stayed behind in town to take care of a few last-minute things, but would meet up with her as soon as possible that evening.

Hailey checked her watch. Time enough for her to take a short nap, have a shower and get dressed. She wanted to look her best.

She was putting the finishing touches on her makeup when she heard a knock at the door.

Smiling, she rushed to answer it.

When she opened the door and saw Nick standing there in a tuxedo looking like a movie star, her eyes widened. She couldn't believe he was hers.

"Wow!" he said. "You look amazing! That dress is really something."

Hailey brushed away a fleck of dust on the long, sleeveless black-velvet dress that fit her figure perfectly. With its low neckline and slit side panel, it was more sophisticated than she normally wore, but Alissa had told her the dress was perfect on her.

"Sorry I'm late. May I come in?" Nick asked. "There's something I want to show you."

"Sure. We've got a little time." She waved him inside and stood by.

He walked into the room, wrapped his arms around her, and smiled at her. "I have a special surprise for you. That's why I couldn't come back to the hotel with you."

"Oh?"

He reached into his pocket, pulled out a couple of photos. He handed her one. "Meet Zeke."

She took hold of the photograph and stared at the picture of a black-and-tan dachshund puppy. Her jaw dropped. "For me?"

He grinned at her. "Yes, sweetheart, for you. A late Christmas gift. I had to drive halfway to Boise to make the deal. We can pick him up together next week."

"Oh, he's adorable! A perfect Zeke. I love him!" Suddenly she was crying—ugly crying with loud, gasping sobs and a flood of tears. "This is … this is … so … so … wonderful! It means so … much to me. Much more than just the puppy. Nick Hensley, I … I …love you!"

"Love you too." He drew her to him and patted her back until she quieted.

"Wait here!" she said. "I have to do my eye makeup all over again. I won't be long."

"Take your time." He picked up the photo and

smiled at the picture of the puppy the kennel owner had given him. He looked at another he'd taken himself and tucked it away.

Several minutes later, Hailey emerged from the bathroom and walked over to where he was sitting on the couch. "There! I think I'm set. But, Nick, I will never forget this lovely gesture. Like I said, it means so much to me."

He rose and kissed her cheek. "Yeah, it means a lot to me too. Wait until you see him! With those bright eyes, floppy ears, and short, crooked little legs, he's really cute."

"I can't wait to meet him!"

"You're going to love him." Nick helped her put on her coat and they left the room.

The party was taking place in the events building, a large, rectangular structure that sat in the opposite direction from the Granite Bar. Nick explained to Hailey it was set up in such a way to accommodate several functions at once using room dividers similar to large ballrooms at big hotels. Tonight, and every New Year's Eve, the entire room would be opened up to hold the crowd that booked months in advance for this special celebration.

The party was exactly like Hailey had hoped. The music, the food, and having her family with her made it perfect. Taking a break from dancing, Hailey gazed at her surroundings with pleasure. Small white-linen-covered tables were set up around a dance floor that backed up to a large stage where a jazz quartet was playing. Wooden beams crossed the high, peaked ceiling and were strung with tiny white lights. Three circling, evenly spaced crystal balls hung from the beams. They reflected the twinkling lights above, sending rainbows of color throughout the space. The effect was breathtaking.

At the near end of the building, a huge buffet displayed an abundance of food, including trays of appetizers and hors d'oeuvres, hams and a steamship roast of beef displayed on carving boards, and an array of assorted vegetables, salads, breads and rolls. Another table held desserts and pastries of all kinds.

Observing the men in tuxes or dark suits and the women in glamorous dresses, Hailey was glad she'd chosen to wear the black dress. She searched for her family and found Jo standing under one of the chandeliers in the midst of the crowd.

Nick turned to greet a friend. While they were talking, Hailey hurried over to Jo.

"Hey! We're still doing our usual New Year's toast with Mom, Stevie and Alissa, aren't we?"

Jo nodded. "We've already talked about it. Everyone is going to try to meet up out on the patio just before midnight."

"Okay, great! See you there!" She hurried back to rejoin Nick.

"Hey! Where'd you go?" he asked.

"I just wanted to make sure my family would all meet for our usual New Year's toast. Just before

173

midnight we'll meet out on the patio. This year, you'll be part of the group," she said, unable to stop a smile from spreading across her face.

"Care for another dance with me?" Nick said, holding out his hand to her.

"Of course. I'd like nothing better," she replied formally, giving him a little curtsey.

Nick led her to a corner of the dance floor and wrapped his arms around her, humming softly as the lush music flowed around them and they swayed back and forth.

They had only a few dances before it was time to join her family for the toast.

Hailey tugged on Nick's arm, "C'mon! We've got to get our glasses of champagne and hurry outside. I don't want to miss having you there for our annual celebration."

He grinned at her. "Okay. Okay."

They each grabbed a glass of the champagne being handed out and stepped outside. Her family was there.

"Twelve ... eleven ... ten ... nine ... eight ... seven ... six ... five ... four ... three ... two ...one!" came the chant from inside and each of them.

At the stroke of midnight, Hailey cried "Happy New Year!"

They toasted one another and then hugs and kisses were exchanged all around.

"Okay," Mom said when everyone had taken a sip. "What's on everyone's mind? Make a wish, set a goal, or make a toast."

Nick lifted his glass. "I'd like to toast Hailey and the baby …"

"You're having a baby?"

"Hailey, is it true?"

As shocked as they by Nick's words, Hailey held up her hand. "What? No! Nick is talking about the baby *dachshund* he's giving me. Show them the picture, Nick. He's so adorable! I've already named him Zeke, like in the Charlie books."

He pulled a photo out from his pocket and handed it to Mom.

"That's my new puppy," said Hailey, her voice trilling with excitement. "We get to pick him up next week. Isn't he adorable?"

"Yes," said Mom, giving her a funny look. "He's truly darling."

"Let me see," said Jo. She took the photo from Mom and studied it. "What's that little black-velvet box next to the puppy?" She turned to Nick. "Is it what I think it is?"

His cheeks turned pink. "What? The box? Oh, damn. That's the wrong photo. Here, this is the correct one." He handed another photograph to her. "Give me the one you have."

"Wait! Hold on. I want to see," said Stevie, taking the photo from Jo. "Oh, I get it. It's a ring box. What's that doing there, Nick? Something you want to tell us?"

"What are you two talking about?" asked Hailey. "It's a picture of Zeke."

"And more, dear sister," said Alissa, giving her a wide smile.

Hailey turned to Nick. "What's going on?"

He knelt in front of her. Taking a small black-velvet box from his pocket, he opened it to show her a beautiful round diamond encircled by a ring of smaller diamonds set in platinum.

"It's not exactly how I'd planned, but Hailey Kirby, will you marry me?"

Hailey's hands flew to her cheeks. She gaped at him and the ring, ignoring the others around them looking on.

He gave her a pleading look. "Well?"

"Yes! Oh, yes! I'll marry you, Nick Hensley! Oh my gosh! This is for real."

His eyes grew moist. "You're the woman I've been looking for all my life. A woman who knows what kindness is and is willing to show others. I want to have a family with you, starting with Zeke. I want to build a life with you, laugh and cry with you. I love you, Hailey. I always will."

She clasped his face in her hands, absorbing his look of love. "I love you too, Nick, for now and forever."

Nick slipped the ring on her finger, stood, and drew her up into his arms.

Hailey felt in a daze as her family applauded.

Mom dabbed at her eyes. "Wow! Even though Hailey told me about her feelings for you, this is definitely a surprise. I've known you since you were a boy, and I wish you both much, much happiness."

"Thanks," said Nick. He turned to Hailey with an apologetic look. "I'm sorry. Like I said, this isn't how I'd planned to propose."

She kissed him on the cheek. "I love having my family here for this special moment. You can ask me again, privately."

He arched an eyebrow at her. "Once wasn't enough?"

She laughed. "I'll never get tired of hearing you say those lovely things about me."

He grew serious. "I meant every word."

Her sisters gathered around her.

"Let's see that ring," Stevie said. She took hold of Hailey's outstretched hand. "I'm so happy for you."

"It's gorgeous, like mine," said Alissa, giving Hailey a kiss on the cheek.

"Lovely," Jo said. "This has been such a special Christmas for all of us."

As the four of them shared hugs, Hailey thought how perfect it was to have her sisters with her for such a life-changing moment.

Lost in a cloud of happiness, Hailey thought back to the time she'd pick up Christmas Kisses as a surprise gift for her family. That was the beginning of discovering the man behind the image, the man she'd agreed to marry. She smiled and gazed up at Nick.

His lips touched hers, and she filled with contentment. These kisses were the most precious gifts of all. She intended to make sure they lasted year-round.

"What are you thinking about? You have a big smile on your face," said Nick, gazing down at her.

"Christmas kisses," she said, knowing with him by her side she could face anything the future might hold for them. She was no longer the scared little girl she'd once been, but a woman in love with the best man she knew. And it felt so very, very good.

EPILOGUE

An Invitation from Hailey

On the morning Hailey was scheduled to go back to work, she climbed out of bed, grabbed a cup of coffee, and sat down on the living room couch where her view through the sliding glass door was of the mountain and Cedar Mountain Lodge. She glanced down at the sparkling diamond on her left hand and sighed with happiness. Who would've thought a vacation that started out with such sadness could have ended this way? Nick Hensley was someone she'd had a crush on as a young girl. Now, as a grown woman, she loved him heart and soul. And, best of all, he loved her too.

She thought of her mother and her sisters—each so precious to her. Christmas had been a special time for each of them, too. So many things going on! It reminded her of her first Christmas with them, learning how wonderful life could be. After all these years, and with everyone living their own lives, she cherished the idea that they were indeed, her soul sisters.

Don't miss the other books in SOUL SISTERS AT CEDAR MOUNTAIN LODGE for a special way to celebrate the holidays. And don't forget your friends! These books make wonderful gifts!

Book 1: Christmas Sisters – perma-FREE prologue book
　　Book 2: Christmas Kisses by Judith Keim
　　Book 3: Christmas Wishes by Tammy L. Grace
　　Book 4: Christmas Hope by Violet Howe
　　Book 5: Christmas Dreams by Ev Bishop
　　Book 6: Christmas Rings by Tess Thompson

Hailey now invites you to enjoy more family stories by reading a sample of CHRISTMAS WISHES, Book #3 of the SOUL SISTERS AT CEDAR MOUNTAIN LODGE BOOKS by Tammy L. Grace in the following pages.

CHRISTMAS WISHES BY TAMMY L. GRACE
CHAPTER 1

Jo's cell phone chimed and she saw her mom's name on the screen. It had taken Jo a long time to refer to Maddie, the woman who adopted her when she was sixteen, as Mom, and she still called her Maddie at times. She had never called anyone else Mom, or at least never remembered doing so. Jo's memories of her birth mother were limited to photos, since she had died before Jo had a chance to know her. From all accounts, she wasn't deserving of the title. She had overdosed and it was never determined if it was accidental or an act of suicide. Regardless of the intent, her mother's death had set Jo on a path that ultimately led to her being in foster care.

Her dad, Joseph, was in the military and had been called back with the sad news. He wasn't in a position to care for a small child on his own, schlepping from base to base. Grandma Maeve, her dad's mother, had come to the rescue, taking Jo in and raising her as her own. Life with her grandmother had been happy and carefree, although she missed seeing her dad. He came home to Granite Ridge a few times each year, but never for long.

Grandma Maeve was the librarian in Granite Ridge and Jo had spent many hours helping shelve books and losing herself within the pages of others. Grandma wasn't rich by any means, but was comfortable and what she couldn't provide in the way of material objects, she more than made up for with the time she dedicated to Jo.

Being an only child, Jo spent most of her free time with adults, and having Grandma for a guardian meant she spent it with more mature adults. She credited that and all the hours she spent reading, with her robust vocabulary and quick mind, not to mention her even quicker tongue. Often, Grandma had to remind her she was not an adult and while she was free to have opinions, not everyone was as open or interested in them as Grandma. That may have explained Jo's lack of close friends during her school years. She had no interest in their juvenile pursuits and elected to spend time with Grandma Maeve and her friends or with her imaginary friends in books.

Then, soon after Jo's eighth birthday, the day military families dread, arrived. Grandma Maeve received the news that her only son, Joseph Daniel O'Malley, had been killed in action. The loss of her son was hard on her, but she and Jo persevered, got through the funeral, and moved on with their lives.

Six years later, when Grandma Maeve suddenly

died, that's when Jo's world began to unravel. There were no other relatives to turn to and Jo was relegated to the foster system. She had endured a year of living with strangers, the last of whom were eventually deemed unfit, thanks to Jo's own intervention. Nobody seemed to care or listen to her when she wrote letters and aired her concerns. She still remembered portly old Mrs. Wacker, her social worker, who was better fit for a job behind a counter in a shop or as a telemarketer, where her actions or more likely lack of such, wouldn't impact any living thing.

Things changed when Jo was taken to Mrs. Kirby's house right before Christmas that first year. Unsure if it would last, but hoping the kind woman's home would be more than just a temporary holiday placement, Jo met the three younger girls – Stevie, Alissa, and Hailey. The women she now called her sisters. That first Christmas, Maddie explained they would be soul sisters and the bond they felt would always be theirs.

Seeing that one word on her phone, "Mom", brought all those old memories rushing back to Jo. The call wasn't unexpected. With Alissa's wedding scheduled for Christmas Eve, Jo's phone had been pinging with texts from her sisters and mom for the last several weeks, checking on details.

Jo had picked up her long silvery gray bridesmaid dress on her lunch hour and it was hanging on the back of her office door, along with the matching sparkly shoes and soft faux fur wrap she had purchased. Maddie had been concerned she might forget the dress, so Jo smiled when she answered.

"I have the dress and my shoes. I'm looking at them right now. No need to worry." Jo glanced at the framed photo on her desk and reached to touch the smooth metal. Although the quality of the photo wasn't great, Jo treasured it. It had been with her for fifteen years and she remembered that feeling when Maddie hugged them all close and snapped the photo on her phone. The smiling faces of her sisters with their mom in the midst, even all these years later, brough a smile to her face.

"Oh, sweetie, I wish this was a call just to nag you about that. Um, I've got some bad news." Maddie's normally enthusiastic voice cracked.

"What's wrong? What's happened?" Jo's forehead creased with worry and she poised her pen over her notepad, tapping it on the paper.

"Jed called off the wedding. Alissa is devastated and heartbroken. She's not up to talking to everyone about it just yet. She also feels guilty, since there's no way to get our money back on anything."

Jo had sent a sizeable check to help with the costs when Jed's family, owners of a very lucrative spirits company in Seattle, had refused to be involved and had in essence boycotted the entire event. Maddie and the other three sisters insisted they would pitch in and help to make sure Alissa had the wedding of her dreams. Maddie and Nan did the bulk of the heavy lifting, but Jo's career afforded her the luxury of being able to cover a substantial amount of the costs and she had been happy to help.

The pen Jo was holding beat faster, pounding the notepad with sharp whacks. Jo had a whisper of a bad feeling about this from the beginning, when she learned that despite their wealth, Jed's parents would not contribute or help in any way. She knew Alissa had been deemed an ill fit for their golden only child. They must have upped the pressure they had been applying to Jed and he cracked.

"Poor Alissa. I can't believe he would wait until now to end it. He must know nothing is refundable at this late date. Although, when you're used to working with billions, what's a few thousand? Especially when it's not your money. We could probably sue him and recoup some of it."

Jo listened to Maddie's deep sigh. "Whoa, let's not go down that road. I've assured Alissa the money doesn't matter, so don't bring it up. She feels bad enough already. Could you call Stevie and let her know? Maybe use your influence to keep her calm. Goodness knows what she'll think is an appropriate reaction. She's liable to show up at Jed's house with a baseball bat or something. This is such a sad and disappointing turn of events."

"Yeah, I'll call Stevie. Don't worry."

"Listen, you've already got time off and your ticket booked. It's been forever since you've spent more than a few days with all of us. Alissa is here. I think we should go ahead up to Cedar Mountain Lodge and stay for the holidays, like we planned.

Take time, let Alissa lick her wounds, surrounded by her family. We could enjoy all the fun activities going on up at the lodge. Do whatever we want, have some downtime, enjoy the gorgeous setting, and the fun New Year's Eve party they always host. It's all paid for and I think we might as well enjoy it."

Jo heard the longing and uptick in Maddie's voice, full of hope. She was worried about Alissa and wanted all her chicks back in the nest, together for her sake and Alissa's. Maddie was right, Jo had been laser focused on her career at Hale and Gray, moving up in the ranks, living carefully, and socking away most of her salary in her investment accounts. This was the first actual vacation she had scheduled. She took a few days off her and there, when Stevie showed up to visit, out of the blue, with her motorhome, or when Alissa came over the summer, but never two weeks off away from the city.

Sometimes, Jo felt like she and Maddie co-parented the other three girls. Jo was the oldest, thirty this year, and like Grandma Maeve used to say, she had been born an old soul. Most people that worked with her or met her, assumed she was a least ten years older. It wasn't due to her appearance, but her serious nature and wisdom beyond her years.

Jo had spent the least amount of time with Maddie and although ashamed of it, was sometimes jealous of the other girls, who had the benefit of being with her for so much longer. Hailey still lived in Granite Ridge, so she got to see Maddie all the time. Alissa was in

Seattle and could make the short trip for a weekend visit. Stevie traveled for seasonal cooking work at various resorts, but came home to Granite Ridge often. Jo was the only one who lived so far away from home. She had been an excellent student and with Maddie's help and nurturing she excelled further and secured a scholarship to college, went on to obtain her law degree, and enjoyed success at the firm she had been with since law school.

That same drive that pushed Jo to be self-reliant at fifteen, was still with her and her quest for a secure future, one where she wouldn't have to rely on anyone, consumed her and left little time for a social life. Any time she had away from her office, was spent at Love Links, the organization where Jo volunteered to help foster children and where she felt the most gratified, using her legal skills to help those who needed them most.

Losing Grandma Maeve and being at the mercy of the system had left Jo with not just a desire, but more of a crusade to embark on a career that would allow her to amass wealth and secure her future. She had gained a family, sisters, a mom, even a grandma in Maddie's mother, Nan, but she would never again be reliant on anyone but herself.

She had been looking forward to this trip, the chance to visit with everyone, be surrounded by the love of her sisters and Mom. "I think that sounds great. I've been looking forward to relaxing for two weeks." Jo glanced at the dress. "I guess there's no point in bringing the dress and all the paraphernalia that goes with it?"

"Sadly, the dress won't be needed. I know that won't break your heart, since you're not one that likes to dress up in fancy clothes. You can kick back and relax, enjoy a well-deserved vacation. I can't wait to see you and have all my girls together again."

Jo promised to make the call to Stevie, confirmed she'd meet up with everyone at the lodge the day after tomorrow, and disconnected.

She took a deep breath and scrolled to Stevie's name. Looking at the time, she realized she only had a few minutes before a meeting. She poked the green button and listened to Stevie's voicemail greeting. Instead of a message, Jo tapped out a text.

Mom just called and said Jed cancelled the wedding. Before you decide to do anything rash, think of Alissa and Mom. Alissa is struggling and very upset. We don't need to do anything that will make her feel worse. Mom thinks we should all go ahead as planned and stay at the lodge over the holidays. I agree and am looking forward to seeing you all the day after tomorrow. We can cheer Alissa up and have a nice long visit. Bonus: I don't have to wear the dress! Heading to a meeting, talk soon. Love you, Jo.

Jo plucked the file from her desk, took her notepad, and left her cell phone. As she walked down the hall to the conference room, she hoped Stevie would heed her words and not do or say anything to exacerbate the situation. Who was she kidding? Stevie wasn't known for her subtlety.

ACKNOWLEDGMENTS

I wish to thank Ev Bishop, Tammy Grace, Violet Howe, and Tess Thompson for including me and my work in this group of sweet Christmas books. I met them by chance at a conference in 2019 and quickly connected with them over the idea of creating a series of short books, writing about sisters of the heart. Working on the books has been a learning experience for me because I usually write longer women's fiction, and I, like the others, have had the challenge of making the books mesh. In working together, I've grown to love these wonderful writers who I think of my very own soul sisters.

I hope you enjoy these stories for the holidays and all year round. If so, be sure and share the news with your friends. Have a wonderful holiday season!

Below are all the books. They make wonderful gifts!

Judith Keim enjoyed her childhood and young-adult years in Elmira, New York, and now makes her home in Boise, Idaho, with her husband and their two dachshunds, Winston and Wally, and other members of her family.

While growing up, she was drawn to the idea of writing stories from a young age. Books were always present, being read, ready to go back to the library, or about to be discovered. All in her family shared information from the books in general conversation, giving them a wealth of knowledge and vivid imaginations.

A hybrid author who both has a publisher and self-publishes, Ms. Keim writes best-selling, heart-warming novels about women who face unexpected challenges, meet them with strength, and find love and happiness along the way. Her best-selling books are based, in part, on many of the places she's lived or visited and on the interesting people she's met, creating believable characters and realistic settings her many loyal readers love. Ms. Keim loves to hear from her readers and appreciates their enthusiasm for her stories.

"I hope you've enjoyed this book. If you have, please help other readers discover it by leaving a review on the site of your choice. And please check out my other books available on all sites. I'm pleased to announce that all my books are now available in audio on iTunes. "So fun to have these characters come alive!" Audio samples of my books are available on my website. You can contact me there. **www.judithkeim.com.**

To like her author page on Facebook: **http://bit.ly/2cfuAEh**

To learn about new books, follow her on Book Bub - **http://bit.ly/2pZBDXq**

And here's a link to where you can sign up for her periodic newsletter! http://bit.ly/2OQsb7s

She is also on Twitter @judithkeim, LinkedIn, and Goodreads. Come say hello!

Note: As part of her participation in the Soul Sisters at Cedar Mountain Lodge series, Ms. Keim is part of the Facebook Group: Soul Sisters Book Chat. To learn more about the five authors and to share friendship and fun with other readers, join here: **https://www.facebook.com/groups/soulsistersbookchat**